January 1990
Sullivan

JOHN
CREASEY'S
CRIME
COLLECTION 1986

JOHN CREASEY'S
CRIME
COLLECTION 1986

Edited by Herbert Harris

St. Martin's Press
New York

John Creasey's Crime Collection 1986
ISSN 0890-6173
ISBN 0-312-00109-6

First published in Great Britain by Victor Gollancz Ltd.

First U.S. Edition

10 9 8 7 6 5 4 3 2 1

CONTENTS

ACKNOWLEDGEMENTS

Acknowledgements are due to *Ellery Queen's Mystery Magazine* for "The Flaw" by Julian Symons, "The Wrath of Zeus" by Margaret Yorke, "Did You Tell Daddy?" by Peter Lovesey, "Flight from Danger" by Andrew Garve, "Dead Ground" by June Thomson, "And Turn The Hour" by Peter Godfrey, and "The Steep Dark Stairs" by Ian Stuart; to *A Box of Tricks* (Gollancz) for "The Thirteenth Killer" by Simon Brett; to *Argosy* for "The African Tree Beavers" by Michael Gilbert and "Lady In The Dark" by Victor Canning; to *Saint Magazine* for "The All-Bad Hat" by H. R. F. Keating; to *Woman's Own* for "Time Spent in Reconnaissance" by Ted Allbeury; to *Reveille* for "The Doctor Afraid of Blood" by Herbert Harris; to *Weekend* for "The Last of the Midnight Gardeners" by Tony Wilmot. Original stories are "Truth to Tell" by Penelope Wallace and "The Dead Don't Steal" by Ella Griffiths (Ormhaug), translated from the Norwegian by J. Basil Cowlishaw.

INTRODUCTION

Since *John Creasey's Crime Collection* first made its appearance under the Gollancz banner in 1977, there have been ten such volumes of short stories by members of the Crime Writers' Association, including the present anthology.

During this period, reviewers on both sides of the Atlantic have been generous in their praise, and some have gone so far as to call it the finest anthology of its kind.

I remember with appreciation one tribute in *The Times* which ran: "The best aunts put a bowl of sweet raisins beside the guest-bed: this is it." A particularly apposite comment, because a collection of short stories such as this is surely the obvious choice for the guest's bedside table. Your short-sojourn guest is reluctant to start a book he cannot finish, and the anthology offers one complete story at a time, of differing lengths to suit the needs of the moment.

One particularly gratifying comment came in a BBC book programme in which the reviewer said: "In his introduction the Editor recommends this as the perfect book to place by the bed in your guest bedroom. To hell with the guests—this book is staying by *my* bedside!"

As a "digger-out of good stories in danger of oblivion" (to quote *The Times* again), I have now collected more than three hundred short stories in the twenty anthologies I have had the privilege of editing for the Crime Writers' Association. In each Collection I have tried to maintain the same high standards of stylish writing, shrewd characterization, good plotting, and compulsive readability, and I hope you will agree that in this volume the "old hands" and a few of the "newer hands" have pulled it off again; and that, while this may be the age of the epic novel, our talented crime writers prove time and again that "small is beautiful".

HERBERT HARRIS

THE FLAW

Julian Symons

1

"DRINK YOUR COFFEE."

Celia sat feet up on the sofa reading a fashion magazine, the coffee cup on the table beside her. "What's that?"

"I said drink your coffee. You know you like it to be piping hot."

She contemplated the coffee, stirred it with a spoon, then put the spoon back in the saucer. "I'm not sure it's hot enough now."

"I poured it only a couple of minutes ago."

"Yes, but still. I don't know that I feel like coffee tonight. But I do want a brandy." She swung her legs off the sofa and went across to the drinks tray. "A celebratory brandy. Can I pour one for you?"

"What are we celebrating?"

"Me, Giles, not you. I'm celebrating. But you want me to drink my coffee, don't you? All right." She went swiftly back, lifted the coffee cup, drank the contents in two gulps and made a face. "Not very hot. Now may I have my brandy?"

"Of course. Let me pour it for you."

"Oh no, I'll do it myself. After all, you poured the coffee." She smiled sweetly.

"What do you mean?"

"Just that we've both had coffee. And you poured it. But I gave it to you on the tray, remember?"

Sir Giles got up, put a hand to his throat. "What are you trying to say?"

"Only that if I turned the tray round you'll have got my cup and I shall have got yours. But it wouldn't matter. Or would it?"

He made for the door and turned the handle, but it did not open. "It's locked. What have you done with the key?"

"I can't imagine." As he lumbered towards her, swaying a little, she easily evaded him. "You think I'm a fool, Giles, don't you? I'm not, that's your mistake. So this is a celebration."

"Celia." His hand was at his throat again. He choked, collapsed on to the carpet and lay still.

Celia looked at him thoughtfully, finished her brandy, prodded him with her foot and said, "Now, what to do about the body?"

The curtain came down. The first act of *Villain* was over.

2

"I enjoyed it enormously," Duncan George said. "Is it all right if I smoke?"

"Of course." Oliver Glass was busy at the dressing table, removing the makeup that had turned him into Sir Giles. In the glass he saw Dunc packing his pipe and lighting it. Good old Dunc, he thought, reliable dull old Dunc, his reactions are always predictable. "Pour yourself a drink."

"Not coffee, I hope."

Oliver's laugh was perfunctory.

"I thought the play was really clever. All those twists and turns in the plot. And you enjoy being the chief actor as well as the writer, don't you, it gives you an extra kick?"

"My dear fellow, you're a psychologist as well as a crime writer yourself, you should know. But after all, who can interpret one's own writing better than oneself? The play . . . well, between these four walls it's a collection of tricks. The supreme trick is to make the audience accept it, to deceive them not once or twice but half-a-dozen times, to make them leave the theatre gasping at the cleverness of it all. And if that's to be done, Sir Giles has to be played on just the right note, so that we're never certain whether he's fooling everybody else or being fooled himself, never quite sure whether he's the villain or the hero. And who knows that

better than the author? So if he happens to be an actor too, he
must be perfect for the part.'

"Excellent special pleading. I'll tell you one thing, though.
When the curtain comes down at the end of the first act,
nobody really believes you're dead. Oliver Glass is the star,
and if you're dead they've been cheated. So they're just waiting
for you to come out of that cupboard."

"But think of the tension that's building while they wait.
Ready, Dunc."

He clapped the other on the shoulder, and they walked out
into the London night. Oliver Glass was a slim, elegant man in
his fifties, successful both as actor and dramatist, so successful
that he could afford to laugh at the critic who said that he had
perfected the art of over-acting, and the other critic who
remarked that after seeing an Oliver Glass play he was always
reminded of the line that said life is mostly froth and bubble.
Whether Oliver did laugh was another matter, for he disliked
any adverse view of his abilities. He had a flat in the heart of
the West End, a small house in Sussex, and a beautiful wife
named Elizabeth who was fifteen years his junior.

Duncan George looked insignificant by his side. He was
short and square, a practising psychiatrist who also wrote crime
stories, and he had known Oliver for some years. He was
typified for Oliver by the abbreviation of his first name, *Dunc*.
He was exactly the kind of person Oliver could imagine
dunking a doughnut into a cup of coffee, or doing something
equally vulgar. With all that, however, Dunc was a good
fellow, and Oliver tolerated him as a companion.

They made their way through the West End to a street off
Leicester Square where the Criminologists' Club met once a
quarter, to eat a late supper followed by a talk on a subject of
criminal interest. The members were all writers about real or
fictitious crime, and on this evening Oliver Glass was to speak
to them on "The Romance of Crime", with Duncan George as
his chairman. When he rose and looked around, with that
gracious look in which there was just a touch of contempt, the
buzz of conversation ceased.

"Gentlemen," he began, "Criminologists . . . fellow crime
writers . . . perhaps fellow criminals. I have come tonight to
plead for romance in the world of crime, for the locked-room

murder, the impossible theft, the crime committed by the invisible man. I have come to plead that you should bring wit and style and complexity to your writings about crime, that you should remember Stevenson's view that life is a bazaar of dangerous and smiling chances, and the remark of Thomas Griffith Wainewright when he confessed to poisoning his pretty sister-in-law: 'It was a terrible thing to do, but she had thick ankles.' I beseech you not to forget those thick ankles as a motive, and to abandon the dreary books some of you write concerned with examining the psychology of two equally dull people to decide which destroyed the other, or to looking at bits of intestines under a microscope to determine whether a tedious husband killed his boring wife. Your sights should be set instead on the Perfect Crime . . . ."

Oliver Glass spoke, as always, without notes, fluently and with style, admiring the fluency and stylishness as the words issued from his mouth. Afterwards he was challenged by some members, Duncan George among them, about that conjectural Perfect Crime. Wasn't it out of date? Not at all, Oliver said, Sir Giles in *Villain* attempted it.

"Yes, but as you remarked yourself, *Villain*'s a mass of clever tricks," Dunc said. "Sir Giles wants to kill Celia as a kind of trick, just to prove that he can get away with it. Or at least, we think he does. Then you play all sorts of variations on the idea: is the poison really a sleeping draught? does she know about it? that kind of thing. Splendid to watch, but nobody would actually try it. In every perfect murder, so called, there is actually a flaw." There was a chorus of agreement, by which Oliver found himself a little irritated.

"How do you know that? The Perfect Crime is one in which the criminal never puts himself within reach of the law. Perhaps, even, no crime is known to have taken place, although that is a little short of perfection. But how do we know, gentlemen, what variations on the Perfect Crime any of us may be planning, may even have carried out? 'The desires of the heart are as crooked as corkscrews,' as the poet says, and I'm sure Dunc can bear that out from his psychiatric experience."

"Any of us is capable of violence under certain circumstances, if that's what you mean. But to set out to commit a Perfect Crime without a motive is the mark of a psychopath."

"I didn't say without motive. A good motive for one man may be trivial to another."

"Tell us when you're going to commit the Perfect Crime, and we'll see if we can solve it," somebody said. There was a murmur of laughter.

Upon this note he left, and strolled home to Everley Court, passing the drunks on the pavements, the blacks and yellows and all conditions of foreigners, who jostled each other or stood gaping outside the sex cinemas. He made a slight detour to pass by the theatre, and saw with a customary glow of pleasure the poster: *Oliver Glass in* Villain. *The Mystery Play by Oliver Glass*. Was he really planning the Perfect Crime? There can be no doubt, he said to himself, that the idea is in your mind. And the elements are there, Elizabeth and deliciously unpredictable Evelyn, and above all the indispensable Eustace. But is it more than a whim? Do I really dislike Elizabeth enough? The answer to that, of course, was that it was not a question of hatred but of playing a game, the game of Oliver Glass versus Society, even Oliver Glass versus the World.

And so home. And to Elizabeth.

A nod to Tyler, the night porter at the block of flats. Up in the lift to the third floor. Key in the door.

From the entrance hall the apartment stretched left and right. To the left Elizabeth's bedroom and bathroom. Almost directly in front of him the living room, further to the right dining room and kitchen, at the extreme right Oliver's bedroom and bathroom. He went into the living room, switched on the light. On the mantelpiece there was a note in Elizabeth's scrawl: *O. Please come to see me if back before 2 a.m. E.*

For two years now they had communicated largely by means of such notes. It had begun—how had it begun?—because she was so infuriatingly talkative when he wanted to concentrate. "I am an artist," he had said. "The artist needs isolation, if the fruits of genius are to ripen on the bough of inspiration." The time had been when Elizabeth listened open-eyed to such words, but those days had gone. For a long while now she had made comments suggesting that his qualities as actor and writer fell short of genius, or had pointed out that last night he had happily stayed late at a party. She did not understand the artistic temperament. Her nagging criticism had become, quite simply, a bore.

There was, he admitted as he turned the note in his fingers, something else. There were the girls needed by the artist as part of his inspiration, the human clay turned by him into something better. Elizabeth had never understood about them, and in particularly had failed to understand when she had returned to find one of them with him on the living room carpet. She had spoken of divorce, but he knew the words to be idle. Elizabeth had extravagant tastes, and divorce would hardly allow her to indulge them. So the notes developed. They lived separate lives, with occasional evenings when she acted as hostess, or came in and chatted amiably enough to friends. For the most part the arrangement suited him rather well, although just at present his absorption with Evelyn was such. . . .

He went in to see Elizabeth.

She was sitting on a small sofa, reading. Although he valued youth above all things, he conceded, as he looked appraisingly at her, that she was still attractive. Her figure was slim (no children, he could not have endured the messy noisy things), legs elegant, dainty feet. She had kept her figure, as—he confirmed, looking at himself in the glass—he had kept his. How curious that he no longer found her desirable.

"Oliver." He turned. "Stop looking at yourself."

"Was I doing that?"

"You know you were. Stop acting."

"But I am an actor."

"Acting off stage, I mean. You don't know anybody exists outside yourself."

"There is a respectable philosophical theory maintaining that very proposition. I have invented you, you have invented me. A charming idea."

"A very silly idea. Oliver, why don't you divorce me?"

"Have you given me cause?"

"You know how easily it can be arranged."

He answered with a weary, a world-weary sigh. She exclaimed angrily and he gave her a look of pure dislike, so that she exclaimed again.

"You *do* dislike me, don't you? A touch of genuine feeling.

So why not?" She went over to her dressing table, sat down, took out a pot of cream.

He placed a hand on his heart. "I was—"

"I know. You were born a Catholic. But when did you last go to church?"

"Very well. Say simply that I don't care to divorce you. It would be too vulgar."

"You've got a new girl. I can always tell."

"Is there anything more tedious than feminine intuition?"

"Let me tell you something. This time I shall have you followed. And *I* shall divorce *you*. What do you think of that?"

"Very little." And indeed, who would pay her charge account at Harrods, provide the jewellery she loved? Above all, where would she get the money she gambled away at casinos and race meetings? She had made similar threats before, and he knew them to be empty ones.

"You want me as a kind of butterfly you've stuck with a pin, nothing more."

She was at work with the cream. She used one cream on her face, another on her neck, a third on her legs. Then she covered her face with a black mask, which was supposed to increase the effectiveness of the cream. She often kept this face cream on all night.

There had been a time when he found it exciting to make love to a woman whose face was not visible, but in her case that time had gone long ago. What was she saying now?

"Nothing gets through to you, does it? You have a sort of armour of conceit. But you have the right name, do you know that? *Glass*—if one could see through you there would be nothing, absolutely nothing there. Oliver Glass, *you don't exist*."

Very well, he thought, very well, I am an invisible man. I accept the challenge. Elizabeth, you have signed your death warrant.

3

The idea, then, was settled. Plans had to be made. But they were still unsettled, moving around in what he knew to be his marvellously ingenious mind, when he went to visit Evelyn after lunch on the following day. Evelyn was in her early twenties, young enough—oh yes, he acknowledged it—to be his daughter, young enough also to be pleased by the company of a famous actor. But beyond that, Evelyn fascinated him by her unpredictability. She was a photographer's model much in demand, and he did not doubt that she had other lovers. There were times when she said that she was too busy to see him, or simply that she wanted to be alone, and he accepted these refusals as part of the excitement of the chase. There was a perversity about Evelyn, an abandonment to the whim of the moment, that reached out to something in his own nature. He felt sometimes that there was no suggestion so outrageous that she would refuse to consider it. She had once opened the door of her flat naked, and asked him to strip and accompany her down to the street.

Her flat was off Baker Street, and when he rang the bell there was no reply. At the third ring he felt annoyance. He had telephoned in advance, as always, and she had said she would be there. He pushed the door in a tentative way, and it swung open. In the hall he called her name. There was no reply.

The flat was not large. He went into the living room, which was untidy as usual, glanced into the small kitchen, then went into the bedroom with its unmade bed. What had happened to her, where was she? He entered the bathroom, and recoiled from what he saw.

Evelyn lay face down, half in and half out of the bath. One arm hung over the side of the bath, the other trailed in the water. Her head rested on the side of the bath as though her neck was broken.

He went across to her, touched the arm outside the bath. It was warm. He bent down to feel the pulse. As he did so the arm moved, the body turned, and Evelyn was laughing at him.

"You frightened me. You bitch." But he was excited, not angry.

"The author of *Villain* should be used to tricks." She got out, handed him a towel. "Dry me."

Their lovemaking afterwards had the frantic, paroxysmic quality that he had found in few women. It was as though he were bringing her back from the dead. A thought struck him. "Have you done that with anybody else?"

"Does it matter?"

"Perhaps not. I should still like to know."

"Nobody else."

"It was as though you were another person."

"Good. I'd like to be a different person every time."

He was following his own train of thought. "My wife puts on a black mask after creaming her face at night. That should be exciting, but it isn't."

Evelyn was insatiably curious about the details of sex, and he had told her a good deal about Elizabeth.

"I'm good for you," she said now. "You get a kick each time, don't you?"

"Yes. And you?"

She considered this. She had a similar figure to Elizabeth's but her features were very different, the nose snub instead of aquiline, the eyes blue and wide apart. "In a way. Being who you are gives me a kick."

"Is that all?"

"What do you mean?"

"Don't you like me?"

"It's wet to ask things like that. I never thought you were wet." She looked at him directly with her large, slightly vacant blue eyes. "If you want to know, I get a kick out of you because you're acting all the time. It's the acting you like, not the act. And then I get a kick out of you being an old man."

He was so angry that he slapped her face. She said calmly, "Yes, I like that too."

By the time that night's performance was over his plan was made.

4

In the next two weeks Tyler, the night porter at Everley Court, was approached three times by a tall, bulky man wearing horn-rimmed spectacles. The man asked for Mrs Glass, and seemed upset to learn on every occasion that she was out. Once he handed a note to Tyler and then took it back, saying that it wouldn't do to leave a letter lying around. Twice he left messages, to say that Charles had called and wanted to talk to Mrs Glass. On his third visit the man smelled of drink, and his manner was belligerent. "You tell her I must talk to her," he said in an accent that Tyler could not place, except that the man definitely came from somewhere up north.

"Yes, sir. And the name is—"

"Charles. She'll know."

Tyler coughed. "Begging your pardon, sir, but wouldn't it be better to telephone?"

The man glared at him. "Do you think I haven't tried? You tell her to get in touch. If she doesn't I won't answer for the consequences."

"Charles?" Elizabeth said when Tyler rather hesitantly told her this. "I know two or three people named Charles, but this doesn't seem to fit any of them. What sort of age?"

"Perhaps about forty, Miss Glass. Smartly dressed. A gentleman. Comes from the north, maybe Scotland, if that's any help."

"No doubt it should be, but it isn't."

"He seemed—" Tyler hesitated. "Very concerned."

On the following day Oliver left a note for her. *E. Man rang while you were out, wouldn't leave message. O.* She questioned him about the call.

"He wouldn't say what he wanted. Just rang off when I said you weren't here."

"It must be the same man." She explained about him. "Tyler said he had a northern accent, probably Scottish."

"What Scots do you know named Charles?"

"Charlie Rothsey, but I haven't seen him for years. I wish he'd ring when I'm here."

A couple of evenings later the wish was granted, although she did not speak to the man. Oliver had asked her to give a little supper party after the show for three members of the cast, and because two of them were women Duncan was invited to even up the numbers. Elizabeth was serving the cold salmon when the telephone rang in the living room. Oliver went to answer it. He came back almost at once, looking thoughtful. When Elizabeth said it had been a quick call, he looked sharply at her. "It was your friend Charles. He rang off. Just announced himself, then rang off when he heard my voice."

"Who's Charles?" one of the women asked. "He sounds interesting."

"You'd better ask Elizabeth."

She told the story of the man who had called, and it caused general amusement. Only Oliver remained serious. When the guests were going he asked Duncan to stay behind.

"I just wanted your opinion, Dunc. This man has called three times and now he's telephoning. What sort of man would do this kind of thing, and what can we do about it?"

"What sort of man? Hard to say." Duncan took out his pipe, filled and lit it with maddening deliberation. "Could be a practical joker, harmless enough. Or it could be somebody . . . well, not so harmless. But I don't see that you can do much about it. Obscene and threatening phone calls are ten a penny, as the police will tell you. Of course if he does show up again Elizabeth could see him, but I'd recommend having somebody else here."

This was, Oliver considered, adequate preparation of the ground. It had been established that Elizabeth was being pursued by a character named Charles. There was no doubt about Charles's existence. He obviously existed independently of Oliver Glass, since Tyler had seen him and Oliver himself had spoken to him on the telephone. If Elizabeth was killed, the mysterious Charles would be the first suspect.

Charles had been created as somebody separate from Oliver by that simplicity which is the essence of all fine art. Oliver, like Sir Giles in *Villain*, was a master of disguise. He had in particular the ability possessed by the great Vidocq, of varying his height by twelve inches or more. Charles had been devised from a variety of props like cheek pads, body cushions and false eyebrows, plus the indispensable platform heels. He would make one more appearance, and then vanish from the scene. He would never have to meet anybody who knew Oliver well, something which he slightly regretted. And Charles on the telephone had been an actor whom Oliver had asked to ring during the evening. Oliver had merely said he couldn't talk now but would call him tomorrow, and then put down the receiver.

In the next few days he noticed with amusement tinged with annoyance that Elizabeth had fulfilled her threat of putting a private enquiry agent on his track. He spotted the man hailing a taxi just after he had got one himself, and then getting out a few yards behind him when he stopped outside Evelyn's flat. Later he pointed out the man to Evelyn, standing in a doorway opposite. She giggled, and suggested that they should ask him up.

"I believe you would," he said admiringly. "Is there anything you wouldn't do?"

"If I felt like it, nothing." She was high on some drug or other. "What about you?"

"A lot of things."

"*Careful* old Oliver."

What would she say if she knew what he was planning? He was tempted to say something but resisted, although so far as he could tell nothing would shock her. She suddenly threw up the window, leaned out and gave a piercing whistle. When the man looked up, she beckoned. He turned his head and then began to walk away. Oliver was angry, but what was the use of saying anything? It was her recklessness that fascinated him.

His annoyance was reflected in a note left for Elizabeth. *E. This kind of spying is degrading. O.* He found a reply that night when he came back from the theatre. *O. Your conduct is degrading. Your present fancy is public property. E.*

5

That Oliver Glass had charm was acknowledged even by those not susceptible to it. In the days after the call from Charles he exerted this charm upon Elizabeth. She went out a good deal in the afternoons, where or with whom he really didn't care, and this gave him the chance to leave little notes. One of them ran: *E. You simply MUST be waiting here for me after the theatre. I have a small surprise for you. O.,* and another: *E. Would supper at Wheeler's amuse you this evening? Remembrance of things past . . . O.* On the first occasion he gave her a pretty ruby ring set with pearls, and the reference in the second note was to the fact that they had often eaten at Wheeler's in the early months after marriage. On these evenings he set out to dazzle and amuse her as he had done in the past, and she responded. Perhaps the response was unwilling, but that no doubt was because of Evelyn. He noticed, however, that the man following him was no longer to be seen, and at their Wheeler's supper mentioned this to her.

"I know who she is. I know you've always been like that. Perhaps I have to accept it." Her eyes flashed. "Although if I want to get divorce evidence it won't be difficult."

"An artist needs more than one woman," Oliver said. "But you must not think that I can do without you. I need you. You are a fixed point in a shifting world."

"What nonsense I do talk," he said to himself indulgently. The truth was that contact with her nowadays was distasteful to him. By the side of Evelyn she was insipid. A great actor, however, can play any part, and this one would not be maintained for long.

Only one faintly disconcerting thing happened in this, as he thought of it, second honeymoon period. He came back to the flat unexpectedly early one afternoon, and heard Elizabeth's voice on the telephone. She replaced the receiver as he entered the room. Her face was flushed. When he asked who she had been speaking to, she said, "Charles".

"Charles?" For a moment he could not think who she was talking about. Then he stared at her. Nobody knew better than he that she could not have been speaking to Charles, but of course he could not say that.

"What did he say?"

"Beastly things. I put down the receiver."

Why was she lying? How absurd, how deliciously absurd, if she had a lover. Or was it possible that somebody at the supper party was playing a practical joke? He brushed aside such conjectures because they did not matter now. Nothing could interfere with the enactment of the supreme drama of his life.

6

Celia's intention in *Villain* was to explain Sir Giles's absence by saying that he had gone away on a trip, something he did from time to time. Hence the remark about disposition of the body at the end of Act One. Just after the beginning of the second act the body was revealed by Celia to her lover shoved into a cupboard, a shape hidden in a sack. A few minutes later the cupboard was opened again, and the shape was seen by the audience, although not by Celia, to move slightly. Then, after twenty-five minutes of the second act, there was a brief blackout on stage. When the lights went up Sir Giles emerged from the cupboard, not dead but drugged.

To be enclosed within a sack for that length of time is no pleasure, and in any ordinary theatrical company the body in the sack would have been that of the understudy, with the leading man changing over only a couple of minutes before he was due to emerge from the cupboard. But Oliver believed in what he called the theatre of the actual. In another play he had insisted that the voice of an actress shut up for some time in a trunk must be real and not a recording, so that the actress herself had to be in the trunk. In *Villain* he maintained that the experience of being actually in the sack was emotionally valuable, so that he always stayed in it for the whole length of time it was in the cupboard.

The body in the sack was to provide Oliver with an unbreakable alibi. The interval after Act One lasted fifteen minutes, so that he had nearly forty minutes free. Everley Court was seven minutes' walk from the theatre, and he did not expect to need much more than twenty minutes all told. The body in the sack would be seen to twitch by hundreds of people, and who could be in it but Oliver?

In fact Useful Eustace would be the sack's occupant. Eustace was a dummy used by stage magicians who wanted to achieve very much the effect at which Oliver aimed, of persuading an audience that there was a human being inside a container. He was made of plastic, and inflated to the size of a small man. You then switched on a mechanism which made Eustace kick out arms and legs in a galvanic manner. A battery-operated timer in his back could be set to operate at intervals ranging

from thirty seconds to five minutes. When deflated, Eustace
folded up neatly, into a size no larger than a plastic macintosh.

Eustace was the perfect accomplice. Useful Eustace indeed.
Oliver had tried him out half a dozen times inside a sack of
similar size, and he looked most convincing.

On the afternoon of The Day he rested. Elizabeth was out,
but said that she would be back before seven. His carefully
worded note was left on her mantelpiece. *E. I want you at the
flat ALL this evening. A truly sensational surprise for you. All
the evening, mind, not just after the show. O.* Her curiosity
would not, he felt sure, be able to resist such a note.

During Act One he admired, with the detachment of the
artist, his own performance. He was cynical, ironic, dramatic—
in a word, superb. When it was over he went unobtrusively to
his dressing room. He had no fear of visitors, for he was
known to detest any interruption during the interval.

And now came what in advance he felt to be the only ticklish
part of the operation. The cupboard with the sack in it opened
on to the back of the stage. The danger of carrying out an
inflated Eustace from dressing room to stage was too great—
he must be inflated on site, as it were, and it was possible,
although unlikely, that a wandering stage hand might see him
at work. The Perfect Crime does not depend upon chance or
upon the taking of risks, and if the worst happened, if he
was seen obviously inflating a dummy, the project must be
abandoned for the present time. But fortune favours the
creative artist, or did so on this occasion. Inflation of Eustace
by pump took only a few moments as he knelt by the cupboard,
and nobody came near. The timer had been set for movement
every thirty seconds. He put Eustace into the sack, waited to
see him twitch, closed the cupboard's false back, and strolled
away.

He left the theatre by an unobtrusive exit used by those who
wanted to avoid the autograph hunters outside the stage door,
and walked along head down until he reached the nearest
Underground station, one of the few in London equipped with
lockers and lavatories. Unhurriedly he took Charles's clothes
and shoes from the locker, went into a lavatory, changed, put
his acting clothes back in the locker. Spectacles and revolver
were in his jacket pocket. He had bought the revolver years

ago, when he had been playing a part in which he was supposed to be an expert shot. By practice in a shooting range he had in fact become a quite reasonable one.

As he left the station he looked at his watch. Six minutes. Very good.

Charles put on a pair of grey gloves from another jacket pocket. Three minutes brought him to Everley Court. He walked straight across to the lift, something he could not do without being observed by Tyler. The man came over, and in Charles's husky voice, with its distinctive accent, he said: "Going up to Mrs Glass. Expecting me."

"I'll ring, sir. It's Mr Charles, isn't it?"

"No need. I said, she's expecting me."

Perfectly, admirably calm. But in the lift he felt, quite suddenly, that he would be unable to do it. To allow Elizabeth to divorce him and then to marry or live with Evelyn until they tired of each other, wouldn't that after all be the sensible, obvious thing? But to be *sensible*, to be *obvious*. Were such things worthy of Oliver Glass? Wasn't the whole point that by this death, which in a practical sense was needless, he would show the character of a great artist and a great actor, a truly superior man?

The lift stopped. He got out. The door confronted him. Put key in lock, turn. Enter.

The flat was in darkness, no light in the hall. No sound. "Elizabeth", he called, in a voice that did not seem his own. He had difficulty in not turning and leaving the flat.

He opened the door of the living room. This also was in darkness. Was Elizabeth not there after all, had she ignored his note or failed to return? He felt a wave of relief at the thought, but still there was the bedroom. He must look in the bedroom.

The door was open, a glimmer of light showed within. He did not remember taking the revolver from his pocket, but it was in his gloved hand.

He took two steps into the room. Her dimmed bedside light was switched on. She lay on the bed naked, the black mask over her face. He called out something and she sat up, stretched out arms to him. His reaction was one of disgust and horror.

He was not conscious of squeezing the trigger, but the revolver
in his hand spoke three times. She did not call out but gave a kind of gasp. A patch of
darkness showed between her breasts. She sank back on the
bed. With the action taken, certainty returned to him. Everything
he did now was efficient, exact. He got into the lift, took it
down to the basement and walked out through the garage
down there, meeting nobody. Tyler would be able to say when
Mr Charles had arrived, but not when he left.

Back to the Underground lavatory, clothes changed, Charles's clothing and revolver returned to locker for later disposal,
locker key put in handkerchief pocket of jacket. Return to the
theatre, head down to avoid recognition. A quick glance at his
watch as he opened the back door and moved silently up the
stairs. Nearly thirty minutes had passed.

He knelt at the back of the cupboard and listened to a few
lines of dialogue. The moment at which the body was due to
give its twitch had gone, and Eustace proved his lasting
twitching capacity by giving another shudder, of course not
seen by the audience because the cupboard door was closed.
Eustace had served his purpose. Oliver withdrew him from the
sack and switched him off. With slight pressure to get out the
air he was quickly reduced and folded into a bundle. Oliver
slipped the bundle inside his trousers, and secured it with a
safety pin. The slight bulge might have been apparent on close
examination, but who would carry out such an examination
upon stage?

Beautiful, he thought, as he wriggled into the sack for the
few minutes before he had to appear on stage. Oliver Glass, I
congratulate you in the name of Thomas de Quincey and
Thomas Griffith Wainewright. You have committed the Perfect
Crime.

7

The euphoria lasted through the curtain calls and his customary
few casual words with the audience, in which he congratulated
them on being able to appreciate an intelligent mystery. It

lasted—oh, how he was savouring the only real achievement of his life—while he leisurely removed Sir Giles's makeup, said goodnight, and left the theatre still with Eustace pinned to him. He made one further visit to the Underground, as a result of which Eustace joined Charles's clothes in the locker. The key back in the handkerchief pocket.

As he was walking back to Everley Court, however, he realized with a shock that something had been forgotten. The note! The note which said positively that he would be at the flat during the interval, a note which if the police saw it would certainly lead to uncomfortable questions, perhaps even to a search, and discovery of the locker key. The note was somewhere in the flat, perhaps in Elizabeth's bag. It must be destroyed before he rang the police.

He nodded to Tyler, took the lift up. Key in door again. The door open. Then he stopped.

Light gleamed under the living room door.

Impossible, he thought, impossible. I know that I did not switch on the light when I opened that door. But then who could be inside the room? He took two steps forward, turned the handle, and when the door was open sprang back with a cry.

"Why, Oliver. What's the matter?" Elizabeth said. She sat on the sofa. Duncan stood beside her.

He pulled at his collar, feeling as though he was about to choke, then tried to ask a question but could not utter words.

"Come and see," Duncan said. He approached and took Oliver by the arm. Oliver shook his head, resisted, but in the end let himself be led to the bedroom. The body still lay there, the patch of red between the breasts.

"You even told her about Elizabeth's bedtime habits," Dunc said. "She must have thought you'd have some fun." He lifted the black mask. Evelyn looked up at him.

Back in the living room he poured himself brandy and said to Elizabeth, "You knew?"

"Of course. *Would supper at Wheeler's amuse you this evening?* Do you think I didn't know you were acting as you always are, making some crazy plan. Though I could never have believed—it was Dunc who guessed how crazy it was."

He looked from one of them to the other. "You're lovers?"

Duncan nodded. "My dreary wife and my dull old friend Dunc—a perfect pair."

Duncan took out his pipe, looked at it, put it back in his pocket. "Liz had kept me in touch with what was going on, naturally. It seemed that you must be going to do something or other tonight. So Liz spent the evening with me."

"Why was Evelyn here?" His mind moved frantically from one point to another to see where he had gone wrong.

"We knew about her from having you watched, and all that nonsense about Charles made me think that Elizabeth must be in some sort of danger. So it seemed a good idea to send your note to Evelyn, so that she could be here to greet you. We put the flat key in the envelope."

"The initials were the same."

"Just so," Dunc said placidly.

"You planned for me to kill her."

"I wouldn't say that. Of course, if you happened to mistake her for Liz—but we couldn't guess that she'd put on Liz's mask. We just wanted to warn you that playing games is dangerous."

"You can't prove anything."

"Oh, I think so," Dunc said sagely. "I don't know how you managed to get away from the theatre, some sort of dummy in the sack I suppose? No doubt the police will soon find out. But the important thing is that note. It's in Evelyn's handbag. Shows you arranged to meet her here. Jealous of some younger lover, I suppose."

"But I *wasn't* jealous, I didn't arrange—" He stopped.

"Can't very well say it was for Liz, can you? Not when Evelyn turned up." The door bell rang. "Oh, I forgot to say we called the police when we found the body. Our duty, you know." He looked at Oliver and said reflectively, "You remember I said there was always a flaw in the Perfect Crime? Perhaps I was wrong. I suppose you might say the Perfect Crime is one you benefit from but don't commit yourself, so that nobody can say you're responsible. Do you see what I mean?" Oliver saw what he meant. "And now it's time to let in the police."

THE THIRTEENTH KILLER

Simon Brett

THE WOMAN WALKED into St Mary's churchyard at a quarter past one in the morning on 13 February, and felt the crackle of money in her coat pocket. It was reassuring, but not reassuring enough. Not enough money, in fact. One five-pound note and four ones. The second man had said he only had four, and, since the job was done and he had threatened to throw her out of the car, she had been in no position to argue.

Just two punters—not a lot for a cold night's work. Two depressed kerb-crawlers, desperate for their perfunctory relief. She knew she had been working a bad pitch, but the other girls had been around for a long time and had territorial rights. Most of them had protectors to enforce those rights, too. Couldn't expect it to be easy starting up in a new town.

And she'd had to leave London. The size of the rents had driven her out of Soho, and none of the club-owners were going to offer her anything now her looks had gone. It was ironic to think that only eight years before she'd been Big Tony's girl and queened it at the Salamander Club. But cancer had wasted Big Tony away to nothing, the Salamander had been sold up and reopened as a specialist cinema club, and now she was just a tired old whore trying to make another start.

She'd chosen the town deliberately because of the Thirteenth Killer. Since he'd started his reign of terror, it was said that the girls were keeping off the streets. Meant there might be a chance for someone who was brave enough, or desperate enough, to move in and clean up. She was certainly desperate enough; she tried not to think about the need for bravery.

But nine pounds for a night's work was hardly cleaning up. The rent on her room was 23 a week. And it wasn't even a room she could work from; it was a good couple of miles from the best pickings. Besides, the landlord lived on the premises, and she'd soon be out on her ear if she started bringing men back. She'd tried to get a place in Nelson Avenue, the so-called "Red Light Area," but once again she had been up against a lot of girls with traditional rights. It meant her only chance was working the streets, working in cars, with all the attendant risks.

But she didn't let it depress her. Depression required the exercise of imagination, and that was something she had deliberately curbed all her life. She knew she would survive, and things might get better. That thought wasn't born of optimism—optimism again was a function of imagination—but it was a logical assessment of her chances.

Because now she had another source of income. A chance encounter had opened up new possibilities. Her hard face wrinkled into a smile as her worn-down heels clacked across the path between the tombstones.

She was so engrossed in her thoughts that she didn't see the tall figure detach himself from the yew tree's shadow. Nor did she hear his swift approach across the deadening grass beside the path.

The harsh smile was still on her lips as the brand-new bicycle chain was whipped over her head and snatched tight round her neck. Only a clicking noise came from her mouth as the hands in their blue rubber gloves pulled the chain tighter and tighter.

When she slumped, the tall figure, still maintaining the tension on her neck but keeping at arm's length, started to drag her body across the grass to the yew tree. Here he stopped and continued to pull on the chain with all his strength for a full three minutes.

Then he let the body drop to the ground. She lay dead on her side. He rolled her over on to her back, then the blue rubber fingers deftly straightened the legs and crossed the arms on her chest.

They reached into the pocket of his dark blue jacket and withdrew a polythene bag. From this they extracted a slip of blue paper. It was two inches long and one inch wide, and had been cut with kitchen scissors from a sheet of Basildon Bond Azure notepaper. In the middle of it were three words, typed in capitals by an IBM electric typewriter fitted with a Bookface Academic golf-ball.

The words were "THE THIRTEENTH KILLER".

The woman gaped horribly. Pushing down the swollen tongue with one blue rubber finger, he inserted the slip of paper into her mouth.

He looked round to see that there was no one in sight, checked that he had omitted nothing from the ritual with the corpse, then, keeping in the shadows of the wall, moved silently out of the churchyard.

The body would be discovered in the morning. And, when the police had examined it, there would be no doubt that the Thirteenth Killer had struck again.

At one twenty-five on the morning of 13 February, on the other side of St Mary's churchyard wall, Constable Norton spoke into his walkie-talkie. "Sergeant, just reporting that I've found the front door open at Wainwright's, the newsagents in Lechlade Road. I'm going in to investigate."

The tiny speaker crackled back at him. "Do you want me to get one of the squad cars round?"

"No, don't bother. Mr Wainwright's an absent-minded old sod at the best of times, and when he's been drinking . . . He's forgotten to lock up more than once before now. I'll go in and check. If I don't call again in fifteen minutes, then send a car round."

"Okay. As you know, we want all cars on the alert tonight for . . ."

"Yes, I know, it's the thirteenth. Cheerio, Sarge." The whole Police Force knew it was the 13th, the whole town knew, gradually the whole country was getting to know the date's significance.

The other murders had taken place on the 13th, the first two only a month apart, and then the third after a three-month gap. It had taken three for the pattern to become clear, three before the police got a special "Thirteenth Squad" organized to investigate, three before the press caught on and some reporter managed to extract the name, the Thirteenth Killer, to swell his headlines.

Since then, nothing. Nine months had passed and vigilance

naturally relaxed. The whores were slowly coming out on the streets again. It was Constable Norton's belief that the Thirteenth Killer wouldn't strike again. The increased police effort, the publicity, it had all scared him off.

For nine months every cop in the town had been on the alert, his head ringing with "privileged information". That's what the Superintendent they put in charge of the Thirteenth Squad had called it—privileged information. They all knew about the stranglings with a bicycle chain, the laying-out of the bodies, the macabre message in the mouth on Basildon Bond Azure notepaper, typed by a Bookface Academic golf-ball. They even knew about the blue rubber gloves, which had left traces on the chains.

And they all knew they must never give away any of this privileged information. Not to their wives, not to their lovers, not to their priests, to no one. There was always the danger of some nut trying a carbon copy murder.

Constable Norton didn't expect a carbon copy murder by a nut, any more than he expected another authentic attack. In his view, the case was over, stale and over.

And, increasingly, the rest of the Force was coming round to his opinion. Oh, some of the young ones—like that Constable Tate—they still thought there'd be another. Tate obviously thought he was going to solve the case single-handed, kept volunteering for nights down round Nelson Avenue, even snooping there when he was off-duty. He saw himself as the great hero who was going to nail the bastard. He was young and ambitious.

Norton remembered when he had been like that, when he'd joined the Force and for his first few years in London. Seemed a long time ago. Anyway, he'd had to leave London. And he was better off here. Nice quiet manor most of the time, even a good chance of promotion. Married a few years back, two kids. Not as much money as back in the London days, but safer.

It took him five minutes to reach Wainwright's, the newsagents.

The door was locked, but he had a key that fitted. As he raised it to the lock, he noticed he was still wearing the blue rubber gloves.

They were safely in his trouser pocket when he knocked on Mr Wainwright's bedroom door. The old man took a bit of rousing from his alcohol- and pill-induced slumbers. He opened the door, half-heartedly clutching a poker, still too bleary even to be frightened.

"Don't worry, Mr Wainwright, it's only me, Constable Norton."

The old man grunted, uncomprehending.

"You left your front door unlocked again, you naughty boy."

"Oh. I thought I'd . . ."

"Well, you hadn't. Less of the bottle and a bit more concentration, me old lad, or you'll have all the villains in the area helping themselves to your takings."

"Yes, I . . ." The old man'a head was aching. "What time is it?"

Norton flashed a look at his watch, deducted nine minutes, and said, "One twenty-six."

"Ah. I . . . should I come down and . . . ?"

"No, no, I'll slip the latch, don't worry. You just get back to bed. But don't let it happen again, eh?"

"No, I . . . er . . ." But, given permission to go back to bed, the old man was already on his way. As he slumped under the covers, he mumbled a "Thank you", and immediately started breathing deeply. Norton waited a couple of minutes until the breathing had swelled to snores, and then went back down to the shop.

That's the advantage of being a good cop, he thought wryly—knowing all the people on your manor, knowing who drinks too much, who's on sleeping pills, who's likely to be a bit vague about time.

He slipped the latch on the door and checked it was firmly locked, then looked at his watch. Twelve minutes since his last call to the station.

"Sergeant, Constable Norton. All okay at Wainwright's. As I thought, old fool had been hitting the bottle and forgot to lock up. So I gave him a telling-off and he's gone back to bed."

"Okay, Norton. Thanks for calling in. And don't forget, it's the thirteenth. Keep a look-out for . . ."

"Yes, Sarge, of course, Sarge." A brief pause. "You know, I don't think it's going to happen again."

"Don't tell anyone on the Thirteenth Squad, Norton, but, actually, neither do I."

As he paced his beat, Constable Norton went through what he had to do. The main thing was to keep calm, and he didn't think that'd be a problem. He'd been calm enough when he'd pocketed the Bookface Academic golf-ball from that insurance office where there'd been a break-in. He'd been calm enough when he sent his son out to buy a new bicycle chain; and calm enough when he'd said he'd broken it and sent the boy out for another. He'd been calm when he'd asked his wife to buy some rubber gloves for cleaning the car.

Come to that, he'd been calm enough while he killed the woman.

And he knew he'd had to do that. He'd been over the problem many times in the last three weeks, and he couldn't see any other way round it.

He'd thought, when he got transferred from the Metropolitan, he was okay. The bribery enquiries were getting close, but not close enough. He reckoned he got out just in time.

He'd been lucky, too. The only person who could really point the finger at him was Big Tony, and Big Tony had died of cancer just at the most convenient moment. So Norton had started in the new town with a clean slate, and seemed to be making a success of it.

Or rather, was making a success of it until he picked up the woman for soliciting. Her recognition of him had been instantaneous, and she'd come up with far too much detail of meetings at the Salamander Club, dates, times, the sums of money involved. What he'd expected to be a quick trip down to the station to charge her had ended with him pleading and agreeing to a hundred-pound pay-off the next night.

There had been another pay-off each week since then. Three hundred quid. That was a lot on his pay. The wife hadn't yet realized what was happening to their savings; when she did, he'd have to invent some story about losing it on the horses.

But it couldn't go on like that. The woman was likely to get more greedy rather than less. She was used to a lot of money

from her days with Big Tony, and the idea of screwing it out of
a cop was one that would appeal to her.

It was after the first pay-off that he had thought of the
Thirteenth Killer idea, and the more he thought about it, the
better it seemed.

The woman was, after all, an ideal victim. Shiftless, unat-
tached, a prostitute like the others. A second-class citizen, the
sort whom most of the population righteously reckoned invited
danger by her choice of work. No one would mourn her and,
so long as the details of the murder were right, no one would
be suspected, except for the Thirteenth Killer. The press would
have a field day, the whores would go back off the streets for a
few weeks, and one more unsolved murder would join a
sequence that Norton reckoned had already stopped.

So he just had to keep calm, and it'd be all right. Sure, he'd
be questioned, because the murder had taken place on his
patch, but he knew who'd do the questioning and he knew
they'd be sympathetic. The Thirteenth Killer had made a point
of doing the other women in well-patrolled areas, but no one
in the Force wanted to draw attention to this. The police were
already looking silly enough, as the deaths accumulated.

No, it'd be all right.

He didn't think the body would be found till daylight. A lot
of commuters went through St Mary's churchyard on their way
to the station. Norton went off duty at six, so he didn't reckon
he'd be called to the scene of the crime.

The only important thing he had to do was to get rid of the
blue rubber gloves. And that had to be managed with care. He
knew enough about the workings of the forensic boys—once
again his "privileged information" was helping—to realize the
traces he might have left on the gloves, prints, minute hairs, a
whole collection of miscroscopic clues that could link him to
the murder.

He also knew, from his own tedious experience, the detail of
the police searches that would follow the discovery of the
woman's body. To dispose of the gloves anywhere on his beat
would be too risky.

But he had planned for that, too. He felt a glow of satisfaction as he contemplated the extent of his planning.

The gloves had to be burnt. Burnt with intense heat until they congealed, melted, and were consumed.

And they were going to be burnt in the one place where police investigators would never look for them.

He continued evenly pacing his beat.

It wasn't yet light at six-fifteen as he approached the back entrance of the police station. The welcome blast of heat from the antiquated radiators greeted him as he walked inside.

He smiled at the irony. The heating system at the Station had long been scheduled for modernization, but the work kept being delayed. And as long as it was delayed, the old coal-fired boiler remained roaring away in the basement. Right next to the constables' locker room.

All he had to do was go downstairs and slip the gloves under the lid of the boiler. There'd be nobody around. The other constables would have nipped into the locker room sharp at six and already be on their way home or warming up with cups of tea in the canteen.

As he walked along towards the basement stairs, a WPC came rushing along the corridor. "Sensible lad, Norton," she said, "coming in the back way."

"What do you mean?"

"Can't get through the reporters at the front."

"Eh?"

"Haven't you heard? The Thirteenth Killer's struck again!"

And she hurried on.

He assessed how hard the news had hit him. So . . . someone had found the woman's body earlier than he had expected. So . . . his interrogation would come that much earlier.

But it didn't worry him. He still felt calm. He could cope.

Just get rid of the gloves, and he could cope.

He had started down the stairs when Constable Tate came bursting out of the Operations Room. The youth was transformed. He walked ten feet tall and positively glowed with triumph. "Norton," he shouted, "have you heard?"

The urge to get down to the boiler was strong, but Norton curbed it. Act naturally. Act naturally, and everything will be all right.

He managed a wry grin. "Yes, Tate, I've heard. The Thirteenth Killer has struck again. I take it all back. You were right and I was wrong."

"Thank you. Very decent of you to say so."

"So now all that remains is for us to find the bastard."

"But we have!"

"What?"

"Or rather *I* have."

"You . . . ?"

"I was patrolling Nelson Avenue at half-past twelve and I actually saw the attack. Had to chase the bastard for miles, but I got him! Caught him absolutely red—no, get it right—caught him *blue*-handed! Isn't it great news? He's in the . . . Here, are you all right?"

Norton was not all right. The shock hit him like a punch in the stomach and he vomited instantly.

"Good God, you poor soul. Have you got a handkerchief? Let me mop you up."

"No, I . . ."

But Norton was too weak to stop Constable Tate from reaching into the trouser pocket. He just swayed feebly against the wall as the young man drew out the rolled pair of blue rubber gloves.

It was at that moment that everyone came rushing out of the Operations Room with news of another sensation.

A woman's body had been found in St Mary's churchyard.

THE AFRICAN TREE-BEAVERS

Michael Gilbert

LIKE MANY PRACTICAL and unimaginative men, Mr Calder believed in certain private superstitions. He would never take a train which left at one minute to the hour, distrusted the number twenty-nine, and refused to open any parcel or letter on which the stamp had been fixed upside down. This, incidentally, saved his life when he refused to open an innocent-looking parcel bearing the imprint of a bookseller from whom he had made many purchases in the past, but which proved, on this occasion, to contain three ounces of tri-toluene and a contact fuse. Mr Behrens sneered at the superstition, but agreed that his friend was lucky.

Mr Calder also believed in coincidences. To be more precise, he believed in a specific law of coincidence. If you heard a new name, or a hitherto unknown fact, twice within twelve hours, you would hear it again before a further twelve hours was up. Not all the schoolmasterly logic of Mr Behrens could shake him in this belief. If challenged to produce an example he will cite the case of the Reverend Francis Osbaldestone.

The first time Mr Calder heard this name was at eleven o'clock at night, at the Old Comrades' Reunion of the infantry regiment with which he had fought for a memorable eight months in the Western Desert in 1942. He attended these reunions once every three years. His real interest was not in reminiscences of the war, but in observation of what had taken place since. It delighted him to see that a Motor Transport Corporal, whom he remembered slouching round in a pair of oily denims, should have become a prosperous garage proprietor, and that the Orderly Room Clerk, who had sold places on the leave roster, had developed his talents, first as a bookmakers' runner, and now as a bookmaker; and that the God-like Company Sergeant-Major should have risen no higher than commissionaire in a block of flats at Putney, and would be forced, if he met him in ordinary life, to call his former clerk, 'Sir'.

Several very old friends were there. Freddie Faulkner, who had stayed on in the army and had risen to command the battalion, surged through the crowd and pressed a large whisky into his hand. Mr Calder accepted it gratefully. One of the penalties of growing old, he had found, was a weak bladder for beer.

Colonel Faulkner shouted above the roar of conversation, "When are you going to keep your promise?"

"What promise?" said Mr Calder. "How many whiskies *is* this? Three or four?"

"I thought I'd get you a fairly large one. It's difficult to get near the bar. Have you forgotten? You promised to come and look me up."

"I hadn't forgotten. It's difficult to get away."

"Nonsense. You're a bachelor. You can up-sticks whenever you like."

"It's difficult to leave Rasselas behind."

"That dog of yours? For God's sake! Where do you think I live? In Hampstead Garden Suburb? Bring him with you! He'll have the time of his life. He can chase anything that moves, except my pheasants."

"He's a very well-behaved dog," said Mr Calder, "and does exactly what I tell him. If you really want me—"

"Certainly I do. Moreover, I can introduce Rasselas to another animal lover. Our rector. Francis Osbaldestone. A remarkable chap. Now get your diary out, and fix a date. . . ."

It was ten o'clock on the following morning when the name cropped up next. Mr Calder was stretched in one chair in front of the fire, his eyes shut, nursing the lingering remains of a not disagreeable hangover. Mr Behrens was in the other chair, reading the Sunday newspapers. Rasselas occupied most of the space between them.

Mr Behrens said, "Have you read this? It's very interesting. There's a clergyman who performs miracles."

"The biggest miracle any clergyman can perform nowadays," said Mr Calder sleepily, "is to get people to come to church."

"Oh, they come to *his* church all right. Full house, every Sunday. Standing-room only."

"How does he do it?"

"Personal attraction. He's equally successful with animals. However savage or shy they are, he can make them come to him, and behave themselves."

"He ought to try it on a bull."

"He has. Listen to this: *On one occasion, a bull got loose and threatened some children who were picnicking in a field. The rector, who happened to be passing, quelled the bull with a few well-chosen words. The children were soon taking rides on the bull's back.*"

"Animal magnetism."

"I suppose, if you'd met St Francis of Assisi, you'd have sniffed and said, 'Animal magnetism'."

"He was a saint."

"How do you know this man isn't?"

"He may be. But it would need more than a few tricks with animals to convince me."

"Then what about miracles? *On another occasion, the rector was woken on a night of storm by an alarm of fire. The verger ran down to the rectory to tell the rector that a barn had been struck by lightning. The telephone line to the nearest town with a fire brigade was down. The rector said, 'Not a moment to lose. The bells must be rung.' As he spoke, the bells started to ring themselves.*"

Mr Calder snorted.

"It's gospel truth," Mr Behrens said. "Mr Penny, the verger, vouches for it. He says that by the time he got back to his cottage, where the only key of the bell-chamber is kept, and got across with it to the church, the bells had *stopped* ringing. He went up into the belfry. There was no one there. The ropes were on their hooks. Everything was in perfect order. At that moment, the brigade arrived. They had heard the bells, and were in time to save the barn."

Mr Calder said, "It sounds like a tall story to me. What do you think, Rasselas?" The dog showed his long white teeth in a smile. "He agrees. What is the name of this paragon?"

"He is the Reverend Francis Osbaldestone."

"Rector of Hedgeborn, in the heart of rural Norfolk."

"Do you know him?"

"I heard his name for the first time at about eleven o'clock last night."

"In that case," said Mr Behrens, "according to the fantastic rules propounded and believed in by you, you will hear it again before ten o'clock this evening."

It was at this precise moment that the telephone rang.

Since Mr Calder's telephone number was not only ex-directory, but was changed every six months, his incoming calls were likely to be matters of business. He was not surprised, therefore, to recognise the voice of Mr Fortescue, who was the Manager of the Westminster Branch of the London and Home Counties Bank, and other things besides.

Mr Fortescue said, "I'd like to see you and Behrens, as soon as possible. Shall we say tomorrow afternoon?"

"Certainly," said Mr Calder. "Can you give me any idea what it's about?"

"You'll find it all in your *Observer*. An article about a clergyman who performs miracles. Francis Osbaldestone."

"Ah!" said Mr Calder

"You sound pleased about something," said Mr Fortescue.

Mr Calder said, "You've just proved a theory."

"I understand," said Mr Fortescue, "that you know Colonel Faulkner quite well, in the army."

"He was my company commander," said Mr Calder.

"Would you say he was an imaginative man?"

"I should think he's got about as much imagination as a No. 11 bus."

"Or a man who would be easily deluded?"

"I'd hate to try."

Mr Fortescue pursed his lips primly, and said, "That was my impression, too. Do you know Hedgeborn?"

"Not the village. But I know that part of Norfolk. It's fairly primitive. The army had a battle school near there during the war. They were a bit slow about handing it back, too."

"I seem to remember," said Mr Behrens, "that there was a row about it. Questions in Parliament. Did they give it back in the end?"

"Most of it. They kept Snelsham Manor, with its park. After

all the trouble at Porton Experimental Station, they moved the
gas section down to Cornwall, and transferred the Bacterial
Warfare Establishment to Snelsham, which is less than two
miles from Hedgeborn."

"I can understand," said Mr Calder, "that Security would
keep a careful eye on an establishment like Snelsham. But why
should they be alarmed by a saintly parson two miles down the
valley?"

"You are not aware of what happened last week?"

"Ought we to be?"

"It has been kept out of the press. It's bound to leak out
sooner or later. Your saintly parson led what I can only
describe as a village task force. It was composed of the
members of the Parochial Church Council, and a couple of
dozen of the villagers and farmers. They broke into Snelsham
Manor."

"But, good God," said Calder, "the security arrangements
must have been pretty ropy."

"The security was adequate: a double wire fence, patrolling
guards and dogs. The village blacksmith cut the fence in two
places. A farm tractor dragged it clear. They had no trouble
with the guards, who were armed with truncheons. The farmers
had shot-guns."

"And the dogs?"

"They made such a fuss of the rector that he was, I
understand, in some danger of being licked to death."

"What did they do when they got in?" said Behrens.

"They broke into the experimental wing and liberated twenty
rabbits, a dozen guinea-pigs and nearly fifty rats."

Mr Behrens started to laugh, and managed to turn it into a
cough when he observed Mr Fortescue's eyes on him.

"I hope you don't think it was funny, Behrens. A number of
the rats had been infected with Asiatic plague. They *hope* that
they recaptured or destroyed the whole of that batch."

"Has no action been taken against the rector?"

"Naturally. The police were informed. An inspector and a
sergeant drove over from Thetford to see the rector. They
were refused access."

"Refused?"

"They were told," said Mr Fortescue gently, "that if they

attempted to lay hands on the rector they would be resisted—
by force."

"But surely—" said Mr Behrens. And stopped.

"Yes," said Mr Fortescue. "Do think before you say anything. Try to visualize the unparalleled propaganda value to
our friends in the various CND and Peace Groups if an armed
force had to be despatched to seize a village clergyman."

Mr Behrens said, "I'm visualizing it. Do you think one of
the more enterprising bodies—the International Brotherhood
Group occurs to me as a possibility—might have planted
someone in Hedgeborn? Someone who is using the rector's
exceptional influence—"

"It's a possibility. You must remember that the Bacterial
Warfare Wing has only been there for two years. If anyone *has*
been planted, it has been done comparatively recently."

"How long has the rector been there?" said Mr Calder.

"Eighteen months."

"I see."

"The situation is full of possibilities, I agree. I suggest you
tackle it from both ends. I should suppose, Behrens, that
there are few people who know more about the IBG and its
ramifications than you do. Can you find out whether they have
been active in this area recently?"

"I'll do my best."

"We can none of us do more than our best," agreed Mr
Fortescue. "And you, Calder, must go down to Hedgeborn
immediately. I imagine that Colonel Faulkner would invite
you?"

"I have a standing invitation," said Mr Calder. "For the
shooting."

Hedgeborn has changed in the last four hundred years, but not
very much. The church was built in the reign of Charles the
Martyr, and the Manor in the reign of Anne the Good. There
is a village smithy, where a farmer can still get his horses shod.
He can also buy diesel oil for his tractor. The cottages have
thatched roofs, and television aerials.

Mr Calder leaned out of his bedroom window at the Manor
and surveyed the village, asleep under a full moon. He could
see the church, at the far end of the village street, perched on

a slight rise, its bell-tower outlined against the sky. There was a huddle of cottages round it. The one with a light in it would belong to Mr Penny, the verger, who had come running down the street to tell the rector that Farmer Alsop's farm was on fire. If he leaned out of the window, Mr Calder could just see the roof of the rectory, at the far end of the street, masked by trees.

Could there be any truth in the story of the bells? It had seemed fantastic in London. It seemed less so now.

A soft knock at the door heralded the arrival of Stokes, once the Colonel's batman, now his factotum.

"Would you care for a nightcap before you turn in, sir?"

"Certainly not," said Mr Calder. "Not after that lovely dinner. Did you cook it yourself?"

Stokes looked gratified. "It wasn't what you might call hote kweezeen."

"It was excellent. Tell me, don't you find things a bit quiet down here?"

"I'm used to it, sir. I was born here."

"I didn't realize that," said Mr Calder.

"I saw you looking at the smithy this afternoon. Enoch Clavering's my first cousin. Come to that, we're mostly first or second cousins. Alsops, and Stokes, and Vowles, and Claverings."

"It would have been Enoch who cut down the fence at Snelsham Manor?"

"That's right, sir." Stokes' voice was respectful, but there was a hint of wariness in it. "How did you know about that, if you don't mind me asking? It hasn't been in the papers."

"The colonel told me."

"Oh, of course. All the same, I do wonder how *he* knew about Enoch cutting down the fence. He wasn't with us."

"With *you*?" said Mr Calder. "Do I gather, Stokes, that you took part in this—this enterprise?"

"Well, naturally, sir. Seeing I'm a member of the Parochial Church Council. Would there be anything more?"

"Nothing more," said Mr Calder. "Goodnight."

He lay awake for a long time, listening to the owls talking to each other in the elms. . . .

"It's true," said Colonel Faulkner next morning. "We are a

bit inbred. All Norfolk men are odd. It makes us just a bit odder, that's all."

"Tell me about your rector."

"He was some sort of missionary, I believe. In darkest Africa. Got malaria very badly, and was invalided out."

"From darkest Africa to darkest Norfolk. What do you make of him?"

The colonel was lighting his after-breakfast pipe, and took time to think about that. He said, "I just don't know, Calder. Might be a saint. Might be a scoundrel. He's got a touch with animals. No denying that."

"What about the miracles?"

"No doubt they've been exaggerated in the telling. But— well—that business of the bells . . . I can give chapter and verse for that. There only *is* one key to the bell-chamber. I remember what a fuss there was when it was mislaid last year. And no-one could have got it from Penny's cottage, opened the tower up, rung the bells, *and* put the key back without someone seeing him. Stark impossibility."

"How many bells rang?"

"The tenor and the treble. That's the way we always ring them for an alarm. One of the farmers across the valley heard them, got out of bed, spotted the fire, and phoned for the brigade."

"Two bells," said Mr Calder thoughtfully. "So one man *could* have rung them."

"If he could have got in."

"Quite so." Mr Calder was looking at a list. "There are three people I should like to meet. A man called Smedley . . ."

"The rector's warden. I'm people's warden. He's my opposite number. Don't like him much."

"Miss Martin, your organist. I believe she has a cottage near the church. And Mr Smallpiece, your village postmaster."

"Why those three?"

"Because," said Calder, "apart from the rector himself, they are the only people who have come to live in this village during the past two years—so Stokes tells me."

"He ought to know," said the Colonel. "He's related to half the village."

Mr Smedley lived in a small, dark cottage. It was tucked away behind the Viscount Townshend public house, which had a signboard outside it with a picture of the Second Viscount looking remarkably like the turnip which had become associated with his name.

Mr Smedley was old and thin, and inclined to be cautious. He thawed very slightly when he discovered that his visitor was the son of Canon Calder of Salisbury.

"A world authority on monumental brasses," he said. "You must be proud of him."

"I'd no idea."

"Yes, indeed. I have a copy somewhere of a paper he wrote on the brasses at Verden, in Hanover. A most scholarly work. We have some fine brasses in the church here, too. Not as old or as notable as Stoke d'Abernon, but very fine."

"It's an interesting village altogether. You've been getting into the papers."

"I'd no idea that our brasses were *that* famous."

"Not your brasses. Your rector. He's been written up as a miracle-worker."

"I'm not surprised."

"Oh, why?"

Mr Smedley blinked maliciously, and said, "I'm not surprised at the ability of the press to cheapen anything it touches."

"But *are* they miracles?"

"You'll have to define your terms. If you accept the Shavian definition of a miracle as an event which creates faith, then certainly, yes. They are miracles."

It occurred to Mr Calder that Mr Smedley was enjoying this conversation more than he was. He said, "You know quite well what I mean. Is there a rational explanation for them?"

"Again, it depends what you mean by rational."

"I mean," said Mr Calder bluntly, "are they miracles or conjuring tricks?"

Mr Smedley considered the matter, his head on one side. Then he said, "Isn't that a question which you should put to the rector? After all, if they are conjuring tricks, he must be the conjurer."

"I was planning to do just that," said Mr Calder, and prepared to take his leave.

When he was at the door, his host checked him by laying a claw-like hand on his arm. He said, "Might I offer a word of advice? This is not an ordinary village. I suppose the word which would come most readily to mind is—primitive. I don't mean anything sinister. But, being so isolated, it has grown up rather more slowly than the outside world. And another thing . . ." Mr Smedley paused, and Mr Calder was reminded of an old black crow, cautiously approaching a tempting morsel, wondering whether he dared to seize it. "I ought to warn you that the people here are very fond of their rector. If what they regarded as divine manifestations were described by you as conjuring tricks, well—you see what I mean."

"I see what you mean," said Mr Calder. He went out into the village street, took a couple of deep breaths, and made his way to the post office.

The post office was dark, dusty and empty. He could hear the postmaster, in the back room, wrestling with a manual telephone exchange. He realised, as he listened, that Mr Smallpiece was no Norfolkman. His voice suggested that he had been brought up within sound of Bow Bells. When he emerged, Mr Calder confirmed the diagnosis. If Mr Smedley was a country crow, Mr Smallpiece was a cockney sparrow.

Mr Smallpiece said, "Nice to see a new face around. You'll be staying with the colonel. I 'ope his aunt gets over it."

"Gets over what?"

"Called away ten minutes ago. The old lady 'ad a fit. Not the first one neither. If you ask me, she 'as one whenever she feels lonely."

"Old people are like that," agreed Mr Calder. "Your job must keep you very busy."

" '*Oh, I am the cook and the captain bold, and the mate of the Nancy brig*'," agreed Mr Smallpiece. "I work the exchange— eighteen lines—deliver the mail, sell stamps, send telegrams, and run errands. 'Owever, there's no overtime in this job, and what you don't get paid for you don't get thanked for." He looked at the clock above the counter, which showed five minutes to twelve, pushed the hand on five minutes, turned a card in the door from 'Open' to 'Closed', and said, "Since the colonel won't be back much before two, what price a pint at the Viscount?"

"You take the words out of my mouth," said Mr Calder. "What happens if anyone wants to ring up someone whilst you're out?"

"Well, they can't, can they?" said Mr Smallpiece.

When the colonel returned—his aunt, Mr Calder was glad to learn, was much better—he reported the negative results of his inquiries to date.

"If you want to see Miss Martin, you can probably kill two birds with one stone. She goes along to the rectory most Wednesdays, to practise the harmonium. You'll find the rectory at the far end of the street. The original one was alongside the church, but it was burned down about a hundred years ago. I'm afraid it isn't an architectural gem. Built in the worst style of Victorian ecclesiastical red brick."

Mr Calder, as he lifted the heavy wrought-iron knocker, was inclined to agree. The house was not beautiful. But it had a certain old-fashioned dignity and solidity.

The rector answered the door himself. Mr Calder had hardly known what to expect. A warrior-ecclesiastic in the Norman mould? A fanatical priest, prepared to face stake and faggots for his faith? A subtle Jesuit living by the Rule of Ignatius Loyola in solitude and prayer? What he had not been prepared for was a slight, nondescript man with an apologetic smile who said, "Come in, come in. Don't stand on ceremony. We never lock our doors here. I know you, don't I? Wait! You're Mr Calder, and you're staying at the Manor. *What* a lovely dog! A genuine Persian deerhound of the royal breed. What's his name?"

"He's called Rasselas."

"Rasselas," said the rector. He wasn't looking at the dog, but was staring over his shoulder, as though he could see something of interest behind him in the garden. "Rasselas." The dog gave a rumbling growl. The rector said, "Rasselas," again, very softly. The rumble changed to a snarl. The rector stood perfectly still, and said nothing. The snarl changed back into a rumble.

"Well, that's much better," said the rector. "Did you see? He was fighting me. I wonder why."

"He's usually very well behaved with strangers."

"I'm sure he is. Intelligent, too. Why should he have *assumed* that I was an enemy? You heard him assuming it, didn't you?"

"I heard him changing his mind, too."

"I was able to reassure him. The interesting point is, why should he have started with hostile thoughts? I trust he didn't derive them from you? But I'm being fanciful. Why should you have thoughts about us at all? Come along in and meet our organist, Miss Martin. Such a helpful person, and a spirited performer on almost any instrument."

The opening of an inner door had released a powerful blast of Purcell's overture to *Dido and Aeneas*, played on the harmonium with all stops out.

"Miss Martin. *Miss Martin!*"

"I'm so sorry, Rector. I didn't hear you."

"This is Mr Calder. He's a wartime friend of Colonel Faulkner. Curious that such an evil thing as war should have produced the fine friendships it did."

"Good sometimes comes out of evil, don't you think?"

"No," said the rector. "I'm afraid I don't believe that at all. Good sometimes comes in spite of evil. A very different proposition."

"A beautiful rose," said Miss Martin, "can grow on a dunghill."

"Am I the rose, and Colonel Faulkner the dunghill, or vice-versa?"

Miss Martin tittered. The rector said, "Let that be a warning to you not to take an analogy too far."

"I have to dash along now, but please stay. Miss Martin will do the honours. Have a cup of tea. You will? Splendid."

Over the teacups, as Mr Calder was wondering how to bring the conversation round to the point he required, Miss Martin did it for him. She said, "This is a terrible village for gossip, Mr Calder. Although you've hardly been down here two days, people are already beginning to wonder what you're up to. Particularly as you've been getting round, talking to people."

"I am naturally gregarious," said Mr Calder.

"Now, now. You won't pull the wool over *my* eyes. I know better. You've been sent."

Mr Calder said, trying to keep the surprise out of his voice, "Sent by whom?"

"I'll mention no names. We all know that there are sects and factions in the Church who would find our rector's teachings abhorrent to their own narrow dogma. And who would be envious of his growing reputation."

"Oh, I see," said Mr Calder.

"I'm not asking you to tell me if my guess is correct. What I do want to impress on you is that there is nothing exaggerated in these stories. I'll give you one instance which I can vouch for myself. It was a tea-party we were giving for the Brownies. I'd made a terrible miscalculation. The most appalling disaster faced us. *There wasn't enough to eat.* Can you imagine it?"

"Easily," said Mr Calder, with a shudder.

"I called the rector aside, and told him. He just smiled, and said, 'Look in that cupboard, Miss Martin.' I simply stared at him. It was a cupboard I use myself for music and anthems. I have the only key. I walked over and unlocked it. And what do you think I found? A large plate of freshly cut bread and butter, and two plates of biscuits."

"Enough to feed the five thousand."

"It's odd you should say that. It was the precise analogy that occurred to me."

"Did you tell people about this?"

"I don't gossip. But one of my helpers was there. She must have spread the story. Ah, here is the rector. Don't say a word about it to him. He denies it all, of course."

"I'm glad to see that Miss Martin has been looking after you," said the rector. "A thought has occurred to me. Do you sing?"

"Only under duress."

"Recite, perhaps? We are getting up a village concert. Miss Martin is a tower of strength in such matters. . . ."

"It would appear from his reports," said Mr Fortescue, "that your colleague is entering fully into the life of the village. Last Saturday, according to the *East Anglian Gazette*, he took part in a village concert in aid of the RSPCA. He obliged with a moving rendering of *The Wreck of the Hesperus*."

"Good gracious!" said Mr Behrens. "How very versatile!"

"He would not, however, appear to have advanced very far in the matter I sent him down to investigate. He thinks that the rector is a perfectly sincere enthusiast. He has his eye on three people, any one of whom *might* have been planted in the village to work on him. Have you been able to discover anything?"

"I'm not sure," said Mr Behrens. "I've made the round of our usual contacts. I felt that the International Brotherhood Group was the most likely. It's a line they've tried with some success in the past. Stirring up local prejudice, and working it up into a national campaign. You remember the schoolchildren who trespassed on that missile base in Scotland and were roughly handled?"

"Were alleged to have been roughly handled."

"Yes. It was a put-up job. But they made a lot of capital out of it. I have a line on their chief organizer. My contact thinks they *are* up to something. Which means they've got an agent planted in Hedgeborn."

"Or that the rector is their agent."

"Yes. The difficulty will be to prove it. Their security is rather good."

Mr Fortescue considered the matter, running his thumb down the angle of his promiment chin. He said, "Might you be able to contrive, through your contact, to transmit a particular item of information to their agent in Hedgeborn?"

"I might. But I hardly see—"

"In medicine," said Mr Fortescue, "I am told that, when it proves impossible to clear up a condition by direct treatment, it is sometimes possible to precipitate an artificial crisis which *can* be dealt with."

"Always bearing in mind that, if we do precipitate a crisis, poor old Calder will be in the middle of it."

"Exactly," said Mr Fortescue.

It was on the Friday of the second week of his stay that Mr Calder noticed the change. There was no open hostility. No one attacked him. No one was even rude to him. It was simply that he had ceased to be acceptable to the village. People who had been prepared to chat with him in the bar of the Viscount Townshend now had business of their own to discuss when he appeared. Mr Smedley did not answer his knock, although he could see him through the front window, reading a book. Mr Smallpiece avoided him in the street.

It was like the moment, in a theatre, when the iron safety-curtain descends, cutting off the actors and all on the stage from the audience. Suddenly, he was on one side. The village was on the other.

By the Saturday, the atmosphere had become so oppressive that Mr Calder decided to do something about it. Stokes had driven the Colonel into Thetford on business. He was alone in the house. He decided, on the spur of the moment, to have a word with the rector.

Although it was a fine afternoon, the village street was completely empty. As he walked, he noted the occasional stirring of a curtain, and knew that he was not unobserved, but the silence of the early autumn afternoon lay heavily over everything. On this occasion he had left a strangely subdued Rasselas behind.

His knock at the rectory door was unanswered. Remembering the rector saying, "We never lock our doors here," he turned the handle and went in. The house was silent. He took a few steps along the hall, and stopped. The door on his left was ajar. He looked in. The rector was there. He was kneeling at a carved prie-dieu, as motionless as if he had himself been part of the carving. If he had heard Mr Calder's approach, he took absolutely no notice of it. Feeling extremely foolish, Mr Calder withdrew by the way he had come.

Walking back down the street, he was visited by a recollection of his days with the Military Mission in wartime Albania. The mission had visited a remote village, and had been received with the same silent disregard. They had usually been well received, and it had puzzled them. When he returned to the village some months later, Mr Calder had learned the truth. The village had caught an informer, and were waiting for the mission to go before they dealt with him. He had heard what they had done to the informer, and, although he was not naturally queasy, it had turned his stomach. . . .

That evening, Stokes waited on them in unusual silence. When he had gone, the colonel said, "Whatever it is, it's tomorrow."

"How do you know?"

"I'm told that the rector has been fasting since Thursday. Also that morning service tomorrow has been cancelled, and Evensong brought forward to four o'clock. That's when it'll break."

"It will be a relief," said Mr Calder.

"Stokes thinks you ought to leave tonight. He thinks I shall be all right. You might not be."

"That was thoughtful of Stokes. But I'd as soon stay. That is, unless you want to get rid of me."

"Glad to have you," said the colonel. "Besides, if they see you've gone, they may put it off. Then we shall have to start all over again."

"Did you contact the number I asked you to?"

"Yes. From a public call-box in Thetford."

"And what was the answer?"

"It was so odd," said the colonel, "that I was afraid I might get it wrong, and I wrote it down."

He handed Mr Calder a piece of paper. Mr Calder read it carefully, folded it up, and put it in his pocket.

"Is it good news or bad?"

"I'm not sure," said Mr Calder. "But I can promise you one thing. You'll hear a sermon tomorrow which you won't forget."

When the rector stepped into the pulpit, his face was pale and composed, but it was no longer gentle. Mr Calder wondered how he could ever have considered him nondescript. There was a blazing conviction about the man, a fire and a warmth which lit up the whole church. This was no longer the gentle St Francis. This was Peter the Hermit, "Whose eyes were a flame and whose tongue was a sword."

He stood for a moment, upright and motionless. Then he turned his head slowly, looking from face to face in the crowded congregation, as if searching for support and guidance from his flock. When he started to speak, it was in a quiet, almost conversational voice.

"The anti-Christ has raised his head once more. The Devil is at his work again. We deceived ourselves into thinking that we had dealt him a shrewd blow. We were mistaken. Our former warning has not been heeded. I fear that it will have to be repeated, and this time more strongly."

The colonel looked anxiously at Mr Calder, who mouthed the word, "Wait."

"Far from abandoning the foul work at Snelsham Manor, I have learned that it is not only continuing, but intensifying. More of God's creatures are being imprisoned and tortured by methods which would have shamed the Gestapo. In the name of science, mice, small rabbits, guinea-pigs and hamsters are being put to obscene and painful deaths. Yesterday, a cargo of African tree-beavers, harmless and friendly little animals, arrived at this . . . at this scientific slaughter-house. They are to be inoculated with a virus which will first paralyse their limbs, then cause them to go mad with pain, and, finally, die. The object of the experiment is to hold off the moment of death as long as possible. . . ."

Mr Calder, who was listening with strained attention, had found it difficult to hear the closing sentence, and realized that the rector was now speaking against a ground-swell of noise.

The noise burst out suddenly into a roar. The rector's voice rode over the tumult like a trumpet.

"Are we going to allow this?"

A second roar crashed out with startling violence.

"We will pull down this foul place, stone by stone. We will purge what remains with fire. All who will help, follow me!"

"What do we do?" said the Colonel.

"Sit still," said Mr Calder.

In a moment they were alone in their pew, with a hundred angry faces round them. The rector, still standing in the pulpit, quelled the storm with an upraised hand. He said, "We will have no bloodshed. We cannot fight evil with evil. Those who are not with us are against us. Enoch, take one of them. Two of you the other. Into the vestry with them!"

Mr Calder said, "Go with it. Don't fight."

As they were swirled down the aisle, the colonel saw one anxious face in the crowd. He shouted, "Are you in this, too, Stokes?" The next moment they were in the vestry. The door had clanged shut, and they heard the key turn in the lock. The thick walls and nine inches of stout oak cut down the sound, but they could hear the organ playing. It sounded like Miss Martin's idea of the *Battle Hymn of the Republic*.

"Well," said the colonel. "What do we do now?"

"We give them five minutes to get to the rectory. There'll be some sort of conference there, I imagine."

"And then?"

Mr Calder had seated himself on a pile of hassocks, and sat there, swinging his short legs. He said, "As we have five minutes to kill, maybe I'd better put you in the picture. Why don't you sit down?"

The colonel grunted, and subsided.

Mr Calder said, "Hasn't it struck you that the miracles we've been hearing about were of two quite different types?"

"I don't follow you."

"One sort was simple animal magnetism. No doubt about that. I saw the rector operating on Rasselas. Nearly hypnotized the poor dog. The other sort—well, there's been a lot of talk about them, but I've only heard any real evidence of two. The bells that rang themselves and the food that materialized in a locked cupboard. Isolate them from the general hysteria, and what do they amount to? You told me yourself that the key of the vestry had been mislaid."

"You think someone stole it? Had it copied?"

"Of course."

"Who?"

"Oh," said Mr Calder impatiently, "the person who organized the other miracles, of course. I think it's time we got out of here, don't you?"

"How?"

"Get someone to unlock the door. I notice they left the key in it. There must be some sane folk about."

The colonel said, "Seeing that the nearest farm likely to be helpful to us is a good quarter of a mile away, I'd be interested to know how you intend to shout for help."

"Follow me up that ladder," said Mr Calder. "I'll show you."

In the crowded room at the rectory the rector said, "Is that clear? They'll be expecting us on the southern side, where we attacked before, so we'll come through the woods, on the north. Stokes, can you get the colonel's Land Rover up that side?"

"Easily enough, Rector."

"Have the grappling irons laid out at the back. Tom's tractor follows you. Enoch, how long to cut the wire?"

"Ten seconds."

This produced a rumbling laugh.

"Good. We don't want any unnecessary delay. We drive the tractors straight through the gap and ride in on the back of them. The fire-raising material will be in the trailers behind the rear tractor. The Scouts can see to that under you, Mr Smedley."

"Certainly, Rector. Scouts are experts at lighting fires."

"Excellent. Now, the diversion at the front gate. That will be under you, Miss Martin. You'll have the Guides and Brownies. You demand to be let in. When they refuse, you all start screaming. If you can get hold of the sentry, I suggest you scratch him."

"I'll let Matilda Briggs do *that*," said Miss Martin.

Enoch Clavering touched the rector on the arm and said, "Listen." Then he went over to the window and opened it.

"What is it, Enoch?"

"I thought I heard the bells some minutes ago, but I didn't like to interrupt. They've stopped now. It's like it was the last time. The bells rang themselves. What does it signify?"

"It means," said the rector cheerfully, "that I've been a duffer. I ought to have seen that the trap-door to the belfry was padlocked. Our prisoners must have climbed up and started clapping the tenor and the treble. Since they've stopped, I imagine someone heard them and let them out."

Miss Martin said, "What are we going to do?"

"What we're not going to do is lose our heads. Stokes, you've immobilized the colonel's car?"

Stokes nodded.

"And you've put the telephone line out of communication, Mr Smallpiece?"

"Same as last time."

"Then I don't see how they can summon help in under half an hour. We should have ample time to do all we have to."

"I advise you against it," said Mr Calder.

He was standing in the doorway, one hand in his pocket. He looked placid, but determined. Behind him they could see the great dog, Rasselas, his head almost level with Mr Calder's shoulder, his amber eyes glowing.

For a moment there was complete silence. Then a low growl of anger broke out from the crowded room. The rector said, "Ah, Calder. Tell me who let you out?"

"Jack Collins. And he's gone in his own car to Thetford. The police will be here in half an hour."

"Then they will be too late."

"That's just what I was afraid of," said Mr Calder. "It's why I came down as fast as I could, to stop you."

There was another growl, louder and more menacing. Enoch Clavering stepped forward. He said, "Bundle him down into the cellar, Rector, and let's get on with it."

"I shouldn't try it," said Mr Calder. His voice was still peaceful. "First, because if you put a hand on me this dog will have that hand off. Secondly, because the colonel is outside in the garden. He's got a shotgun, and he'll use it, if he has to."

The rector said gently, "You mustn't think you can frighten us. The colonel won't shoot. He's not a murderer. And Rasselas won't attack me. Will you, Rasselas?"

"You've got this all wrong," said Mr Calder. "My object is to prevent *you* attacking *us*. Just long enough for me to tell you two things. First, the guards at Snelsham have been doubled. They are armed. And they have orders to shoot. What you're leading your flock to isn't a jamboree, like last time. It's a massacre."

"I think he's lying," said Mr Smedley.

"There's one way of finding out," said Mr Calder. "But it's not the real point. The question which really matters—what our American friends would refer to as the sixty-four thousand dollar question—is, have any of you ever seen a tree-beaver?"

The question fell into a sudden pool of silence.

"Come, come," said Mr Calder. "There must be some naturalists here. Rector, I see the *Universal Encyclopaedia of Wild Life* on your shelf. Would you care to turn its pages and give us a few facts about the habits of this curious creature?"

The rector said, with a half-smile of comprehension on his face, "What are you getting at, Mr Calder?"

"I can save you some unnecessary research. The animal does not exist. Indeed, it could not exist. Beavers live in rivers, not in trees. The animal was invented by an old friend of mine, a Mr Behrens. And, having invented this remarkable animal, he thought it would be a pity to keep it all to himself. He had news of its arrival at Snelsham passed to a friend of his, who passed it on to a subversive organization known as the International Brotherhood Group. Who, in turn, passed it to you, Rector, through their local agent."

The rector was smiling now. He said, "So I have been led up the garden path. *Sancta simplicitas!* Who is this agent?"

"That's easy. Who told you about the tree-beavers?"

There was a flurry of movement. A shout, a crash, and the sound of a shot. . . .

"It is far from clear," said Mr Calder, "whether Miss Martin intended to shoot the rector or me. In fact Rasselas knocked her over, and she shot herself. As soon as they realized they had been fooled, the village closed its ranks. They concocted a story that Miss Martin, who was nervous of burglars, was known to possess a revolver, a relic of the last war. She must have been carrying it in her handbag, and the supposition was that, in pulling it out to show to someone, it had gone off and killed her. It was the thinnest story you ever heard, and the Coroner was suspicious as a cat. But he couldn't shake them. And, after all, it was difficult to cast doubt on the evidence of the entire Parochial Church Council, supported by their rector. The verdict was accidental death."

"Excellent," said Mr Fortescue. "It would have been hard to prove anything. In spite of your beavers. How did the rector take it?"

"Very well indeed. I had to stay for the inquest, and made a point of attending Evensong on the following Sunday. The church was so full that it was difficult to find a seat. The rector preached an excellent sermon, on the text, 'Render unto Caesar the things that are Caesar's'."

"A dangerous opponent," said Mr Fortescue. "On the whole, I cannot feel sorry that the authorities should have decided to close Snelsham Manor."

THE WRATH OF ZEUS

Margaret Yorke

THE GODS INDEED were angry, Mr Dunn thought as he sat on the hotel balcony, a towel wrapped ruglike round his bare, skinny shanks, for it was chilly in the storm. He still wore his blue-cotton holiday shorts, though the warm weather had been replaced by a day that would have seemed normal in an English September. Beyond the oleanders and orange trees that edged the hotel garden and bordered the swimming pool, the Ionian Sea raged grey, dotted with whitecaps, and the beach, once fringed with golden sand, was now drab-brown, riven where torrents of rainwater had poured down from the hills and into the sea. The water, once so clear, was muddied with stirred-up sand.

Poseidon, Mr Dunn decided as he observed the scene through his binoculars, was demonstrating his power to goad the sea into a wild warning to mere humans.

Earlier, before the storm, the air had been still, heavy with humidity, the sky full of dense purple clouds massing over the mountains across the bay. Then the sky had been rent by bright bars of vivid forked lightning, followed instantly by deafening thunder. Zeus, in his majesty, was displaying his authority beneath which mortal man must quail.

Henry and Mavis Dunn were spending a fortnight on this Greek island, which could be reached only by ferry from a larger one with an airport—though the term "airport" seemed a grandiloquent description for the minimal hutted buildings serving the runway. Each summer the Dunns went abroad, always to somewhere new, and the choice was usually made by Mavis. This year, however, Henry's wishes had prevailed. For years he'd longed to visit this island, steeped in myth and legend. Now it had a large hotel and he had pointed out to his wife that soon it would be fashionable. By visiting it now, they could boast they'd been there before it became part of the regular tourist run. The argument had persuaded Mavis.

Henry woke early each morning and went out onto the balcony of their hotel room to watch the sky grow light under the beneficence of Aurora. As the sky grew brighter, gradually, in all his glory, Apollo would preside over the heavens as the sun shone burningly down. And in the evening the sunsets were magnificent. Even Mavis, drinking duty-free gin on the balcony before dinner, marvelled as the huge, fiery orb dropped rapidly behind the distant mountain, taking only just over two minutes from the time its rim touched the mountaintop. For a few more minutes, streaks of orange and gold would light the sky—then it was dark. There was no dusk in those waters.

When the sun went down, Mavis would go into the bedroom and begin her evening toilet, which even on holiday included much grimacing in the mirror as she examined her wrinkles; the patting of cream into her thin cheeks; then the painting of brows on the pale ridge of skin over her small, button-brown eyes. It took time to select which dress to wear before she was ready to go down to the bar to meet their new holiday friends, Eileen and Bill, with whom they now dined each night, to Henry's relief. It helped with conversation.

Mavis had been a pretty girl when Henry first met her, long ago. She'd worked as a typist for a firm for which he was a traveller—representatives they were all called these days. His nymph he had christened her then. Even as a young man, Henry had enjoyed reading about ancient times—a schoolmaster had caught his imagination with tales of Mycenae and that had begun it all. "Your silly old books," Mavis would say, referring to the rows of volumes he had acquired from second-hand booksellers over the years.

The first time he took her out they went to a concert, but during the interval he discovered that the music bored her so they left. Their next date, and those that followed, had been at the cinema; he'd held her hand in the conspiring darkness, and she'd giggled and squirmed.

They married quickly when war was declared, for Henry was in the Territorial Army and was called at up once. Their brief honeymoon was a disappointment to both, but for the next six years they met rarely. Things would improve after the war, Henry told himself, clasping her resisting body on the station platform before he left for service abroad.

When he returned after four years, Mavis was no longer the plump, curly-haired girl whose photograph he had carried through the western desert and up the leg of Italy and whose rare, stiff letters he knew by heart. But she'd had a tough time, he reminded himself then. Food had been scarce at home; there had been bombs and doodlebugs—though, to be truthful, few had fallen near Mavis, who had found a job in a government department whose offices were moved, for safety, to Wales. It had been dull for her there, though, Henry allowed, and he was grateful that she'd stayed faithful, for so many of his comrades had returned to find that their wives had failed them.

The first years after the war were not easy. Henry had to make up for lost time. He wanted to succeed in the world, and he knew that he must be able to give Mavis the good things of life to preserve their marriage—possessions were important to her.

"I have certain standards, Henry," she'd said, turning down the first flat he'd found—a dark basement one, but cheap.

It would be better when babies arrived, he'd felt. She'd alter then—be warmer, fulfilled. But no babies came, and he seemed to lack the secret of making her content. Her mouth grew thin and hard. She never laughed. He often thought of her girlish giggle, now gone, and sighed.

In time they had a small house, and later a larger one. Since there were no children, Mavis had kept on her job, transferring from one department to another as time went on, and only recently she had retired from a senior position. Henry had done well himself—he'd had to, to keep up with her. He became a keen gardener, thus keeping out of Mavis's way on summer evenings and weekends, and in winter he read a great deal. His little library steadily grew and his interest in Greek mythology revived.

Now he realized Mavis was not a nymph and never had been. Watching her as she painted her face, her hair tinted dark brown and permed into frizzy corkscrew curls, he thought she was more like Medusa, with her hard expression and with snakes for hair. He was a frightened man, for he himself would retire at Christmas and after that there would be no escape from Mavis. Now she devoted to the house the energy that had been channelled into her work. She'd always been neat and house proud, but now she was fanatical. How would he manage at home all day, Henry wondered bleakly, and what would he do for company without the daily colleagues he had spent more time with than with Mavis?

Years ago Mavis had turned the small guest bedroom in their house into what she called his den. There he kept his books and his record player and a transistor radio—she didn't want that sort of rubbish cluttering up her living room, she had said. Henry knew he would be spending much of his time in his den in future. All these years, by avoiding each other during the day, they'd managed to maintain brief conversations over the evening meal and even Sunday lunch, but holidays had been difficult until they learned to diffuse their intimacy by making friends with another couple. (It was Henry who always found the holiday friends. He'd get talking in the bar the first evening to someone he'd already picked out on the plane as looking likely. He was aware they weren't the only pair with a problem.)

He'd take up bowling, he thought. It was a pity he'd never played golf, but perhaps it wasn't too late to learn—then he could spend every day at the club. Still, he preferred the idea of adult-education classes. He might learn to paint, or even to speak Greek. But, inevitably there would still be hours at home and when he thought about the future, Henry panicked.

Among the holiday visitors on the island there were some happy couples. Henry looked wistfully at a pair, not young at all, strolling arm-in-arm down the road to the little town past orchards of pomegranates and swathes of lush bougainvillaea, bright hibiscus and trails of brilliant morning glory. Nature approved of passion, he sighed, knowing little about it. There were nymphs to be seen, too: lovely young girls who lay, almost naked, stretched out on the beach, their oiled limbs surrendering to the sun. When he went into the sea for his swim he met others emerging, long hair wet against small, neat skulls, curving bodies full of promise. He would watch them

covertly, like a schoolboy, for he knew he had missed something wonderful in the arid years of his marriage.

Zeus had had his way with any maiden he fancied, Henry
thought enviously. Age was no handicap to a god. Henry's
own chest bore a light tufting of grey hair and his legs were still
pale despite several days in the sun. Zeus—older than time—
would simply transform himself into some irresistible figure
before conquering the maiden of his choice. Henry picked
out a maiden—well, a damsel—for himself and dreamed of
appearing before her in the guise of a Greek hero, with golden
curls and muscled torso, to carry her off to a cave, where he
would ravish her to their mutual delight. His choice was a fair
girl who toasted herself on a sunbed close to the spot where,
early every morning, Henry laid out his own and Mavis's
towels under a plaited straw shelter on the beach. Here,
between the swims which punctuated his day, he could watch
the girl from behind the cover of his book.

Eileen and Bill shared the shade of their shelter. Occasionally
the two women splashed in the shallows. Mavis was a poor
swimmer and Eileen could manage only a gasping breast
stroke. Bill would coast up and down with some style but short
breath. But Henry swam across the wide sweep of the bay
each morning to the headland opposite, almost half a mile.
There he would haul himself on to a rock, wary of sea urchins
hiding under the seaweed, rest for a while, and swim back,
escaping from his companions and occupying time in a manner
that was not only good for him but pleasant. Some of the way
he would power himself on with a vigorous crawl, but for
much of the distance he would swim slowly on his side, gazing
at the scenery. Above the rocky hilltops was the vivid blue sky
and below were the olive trees on which much of the island's
prosperity was founded, silvery grey in the sunlight.

The day before the storm, Eileen and Mavis had spent some
hours poking about in the little town while Henry and Bill
took a taxi out to a ruined monastery. Eileen, who kept a
dress shop in Sussex, didn't care for ruins, and neither did
Mavis. The women had enjoyed their day, returning with
several parcels. The men had had an agreeable time, too.

Eileen and Bill had an air bed on which Eileen would paddle

herself for some distance on the calm blue water. Mavis, encouraged to take her turn on the bed, paddled too, and found it was easy enough to move the light mattress and guide it with the movement of her hands. Henry supposed it was safe enough out here where the sea was so calm, though he knew such beds were dangerous in British waters.

Each afternoon, however, no matter how calm and still the sea was in the morning, a sharp breeze blew up and the sailboard riders would come out, their little craft dancing like ballerinas on the small waves. And now there was a storm.

It would pass, Henry thought, as he watched the lightning stab the sky and heard the thunder overhead. Calm would return when the gods were appeased. Did they demand a sacrifice? he wondered.

The next day, the storm had died down and the sky was washed clear of cloud. The swimming pool, filled with twigs and sand swept down by the rain, was drained and cleaned. The tourists went down to the beach again to resume their sybaritic routine.

For three more days it was calm and sunny, but then the air grew still and humid once more. The sea was like glass and Henry went off for his morning swim while the good weather held. He struck out strongly across the bay toward his landmark at the tip of the headland and scrambled out for his rest. But he stayed a shorter time than usual when he saw the sky grow darker. As he swam back, a slight swell caught him halfway across the bay. It was like the wash from a boat. He glanced round, expecting to see a waterskier, though he had heard no motor boat. He saw no craft near enough to have caused the movement of the water, which was odd.

He swam on towards the straw-topped shades on the distant beach, putting his head down and going into a powerful crawl that moved him fast through the water, looking up from time to time to make sure his direction was correct. Some way ahead, a good distance from the shore, he saw an airbed, and just as he noticed it a big wave came up behind him, wrapping itself around him. Henry, a good and confident swimmer, rode the wave safely, but he saw it sweep on toward the airbed. The mattress bobbed up with the wave and Henry wondered who was on it and if it was Eileen's bed. He swam on and made out the bright colour of Mavis's cerise two-piece swimsuit.

Then another wave caught him, a much bigger one than its forerunner. It engulfed him totally, and when he had swum through it he saw it roll towards the air bed.

Poseidon he pleaded, Poseidon—great god of the sea—free me of her. And, as he willed the elements, he saw the air bed, caught by the wave, tip up and throw the woman on it into the water.

As he swam toward the spot, Henry understood what had caused the waves. An earthquake had struck this island years ago, and the area was subject to earth tremors. A tremor somewhere out at sea had made the wave. Drawing nearer, Henry could see a head bobbing in the water. Mavis would panic. She wouldn't be able to swim to the shore and he thought it unlikely that she'd be able to clamber back on to the mattress. He swam powerfully on, and as he drew near another wave came. There was no time to reflect. Poseidon had answered his prayer. Henry took a deep breath and dived into the wave as it bore down on the bobbing head. He grabbed the woman and dragged her beneath the wave with him, forcing her head down and holding it submerged, fighting the natural buoyancy of the salt water to keep her under long enough to make of her the sacrificial offering demanded by the gods, his own lungs bursting with the effort. She struggled and kicked, then finally went limp. At last he surfaced, still holding her. Then he felt Zeus, in vengeance, send a shaft of agony through his own chest.

A man swimming with a snorkel mask and flippers fished the woman's body from the water. Henry was pulled out later, hauled aboard the dinghy that shepherded the sail-board riders.

His death was ruled a massive heart attack while attempting to save a friend—for the woman's body was Eileen's. She had been wearing a cerise swimsuit she had borrowed from the victim's wife. Perhaps, it was conjectured, he had mistaken her for his wife, had been attempting to save his wife.

Mavis received a good deal of sympathy, together with Henry's insurances, which brought with them a very comfortable pension, so that she was able to continue to live up to the considerable standards she had set for them both.

DID YOU TELL DADDY?

Peter Lovesey

JONATHAN WILDING, FOUR years old, his tight curls bleached by the August sun, stepped busily through the village delivering letters. He called at every house. They were his mother Sally's love letters.

Jonathan had found them at the bottom of the spare-room wardrobe when he had gone to look for a tennis ball to replace the one he had lost over next door's wall. The moment he had slipped the elastic band off the shoe-box and lifted the lid, he had forgotten about the ball. Those bundles of letters neatly tied with coloured ribbon had seemed provided for him to realize the one ambition of his young life: to be a postman. Mr Halliwell, with his peaked hat, grey uniform, bicycle and, above all, the brown bag stuffed with letters and parcels, was Jonathan's idol, a loud-voiced, bearded man with something to say to everyone he met, including the children. Sometimes he allowed Jonathan to walk along the street with him and guard the bicycle when he propped it against someone's gatepost.

Jonathan's status this afternoon was infinitely more important. With his nursery-school satchel slung from one shoulder and filled with letters, he made his way purposefully from door to door making his special delivery. He knew that ideally the envelopes should not have been torn open at the top, but every one had a long letter inside, often running to several pages, so no one ought to feel dissatisfied. By a happy chance, there were just enough letters to go round. He had covered both sides of the street, slipping two or three through the doors of people who were particular friends of the family, and he was home and watching television before the first knock came at the front door.

Sally Wilding was in the kitchen cooking plaice and chips for her husband Bernard, the author of the letters. Bernard was asleep upstairs. He was a sergeant in the police, with responsibility for one small town and seven villages, including their own, and this week he was on nights. He and Sally had lived in the village all their lives. It was often mentioned that they had been childhood sweethearts, but that was sentimental blurring of the truth. They had ignored each other in school and avoided each other outside until a month before Bernard had become a police cadet. That month, April 1969, had made nonsense of all the years before. Out of nowhere, an avalanche of passion had engulfed them. They had been eighteen and in love and facing separation, for Bernard had been due to report to Hendon Police College, two hundred miles away, on May 1st. That last weekend, they had got engaged and promised to send letters to each other every day.

Such letters! Sally still blushed at their frankness and prickled with secret pleasure at the unrestraint of Bernard's ardour. If she ever needed a testimony to the force of his passion, it was there in his neatly upright handwriting, more candid and more eloquent than he had been before or since. There had been a few times in their marriage—very few—when she had been glad to take out those letters and read them for reassurance. Bernard was almost certainly unaware that she had kept them.

She heard the doorbell.

"Michael, see who it is, please."

Michael was her first-born, ten years old and pleased to be the man of the house when Bernard was not available.

"It's Mrs Nugent. She wants to speak to you."

Sally sighed, took the frying-pan off the gas, wiped her hands and went to see what the village do-gooder wanted this time. Probably collecting for something. Why was it always when the evening meal was on the go?

"I rather think this belongs to you, my dear."

Sally took the letter and stared at it, unable yet to make the mental leap that linked it with the embarrassed neighbour on her doorstep.

"Somebody pushed it through my door. I expect they got the numbers mixed. It was already open. I haven't looked inside, believe me."

Sally went numb. She couldn't summon the words to respond

to Mrs Nugent. If a chasm had opened between them, she would have jumped into it at once.

Her mind mobilized at last. Which letter was it, for heaven's sake? What was in it? How could it possibly . . . ?

One of the boys!

Fast as her brain began to race, events outpaced it. Mr Marsh from across the street came up the path with two more letters in his hand.

She took them, managed to blurt out something approximating to thanks, closed the door and dashed upstairs to the spare room to have her worst fears confirmed: the shoe-box empty except for one elastic band and three lengths of ribbon.

"Michael, Jonathan! Come here this minute!"

"There's someone else at the door, Mummy."

The reckoning would have to wait. And so would Bernard's dinner.

The front door stood open for the next twenty minutes as Sally's letters were returned to her by a succession of blushing, grinning or frowning neighbours. Some cheerfully admitted having read the letters. For Sally, the ordeal was worse than a day in the stocks.

"I expect it was one of the children," suggested the vicar's wife. "Little scamps. What will they think of next?"

From upstairs, Bernard called out, "Sally, are you there? You didn't call me. Is anything the matter?"

She nodded to the vicar's wife, closed the door and called upstairs, "Sorry, darling. People at the door. You'd better hurry."

She scooped up the letters from the hall table, hurried back into the kitchen and thrust them into the drawer with the teacloths just before Bernard came down.

"Who was it?"

"Oh, just about everybody. I'll tell you later. I'm afraid the chips are ruined, but the fish is still all right."

"I'll have some bread with it. One of the boys up to some mischief?"

"I honestly don't know."

"Want to deal with it yourself?"

Sally nodded.

The doorbell rang again.

"Oh, no!"

She answered it. Miss Sharp, the doctor's receptionist, with two more letters.

Sally returned to the kitchen.

"Letters as late in the day as this?"

She whisked them into the drawer. "Old ones. Got to keep the place tidy." It was hateful deceiving him, but she couldn't face the eruption when he found out. He set high standards for himself, and he expected his family to follow.

He picked up his tunic. "If there's trouble, you can bet your life it's Jonathan. Time we stopped treating him as the baby of the family. He's got to learn."

Sally agreed. Bernard had been more strict with Michael than ever he had been with Jonathan. It showed. Michael was dependable, a quiet, self-sufficient lad with a good capacity for concentration. He liked reading, stamps and model-making. If he misbehaved, it was generally because he put a higher priority on his hobbies than cleaning teeth or tidying his room.

Jonathan was the adventurous one, and naughty with it. He had more than his share of personal charm, which he exploited to the limit.

As soon as Bernard had left for work, Sally questioned Michael. She had always tried to treat the boys even-handedly, even though they responded differently.

"Michael, what were you doing this afternoon?"

"I was at school."

"After that."

"I came home."

"Straight home?"

"Yes."

"What did you do when you came in?"

"Looked at my stamps."

"You didn't go to the spare room for anything?"

"No, Mummy."

Jonathan, when Sally spoke to him, cheerfully admitted playing postman with her letters. He told her everything. Five minutes later, he was in bed with his bottom smarting.

Downstairs, Sally took out the letters. Two more were returned during the evening. She had decided to destroy them all. She could never read them again without being conscious that the words meant only for her had been looked at by others. First, she needed to be sure that they had all come back. She sorted them into sequence. She had never counted them, but she knew Bernard had written her two a week for the whole of his cadet course.

One was missing: the first in the first week of July.

She soon recalled it, by glancing at the next one. Bernard had been waiting for the mid-course tests to be assessed. Keyed up, perhaps, he had poured out his desire for her in a long letter that was a kind of prose-poem to her physical attractions, a mixture of recollection and speculation that she had found wickedly delightful at the time, but now painfully embarrassing.

Which of her neighbours had got the letter and not returned it?

She mentally reviewed everyone who had called, and then in her mind's eye went up and down the village street, checking the houses and their inmates. When she came to Primrose Cottage she stopped. Ruby Simmons. Ruby had not returned a letter.

Ruby was Sally's age. They had gone through school together, but they had never been friends. In those days, Ruby had been an outrageous flirt, the first in their year to appear in eye-shadow and a smear of lipstick, and the leader in every other step towards maturity. The boys had fought battles in the playground over her and she had rewarded them with favours in the cycle shed that were whispered about with sly smiles and sniggers. Sally, who could only guess, had disliked everything about her.

Worse, Ruby had been Bernard's girl for nearly a year before he fell for Sally. This was after they had all left school. Ruby had bleached her carroty-red hair and Bernard had succumbed as if he had never seen a blonde before. She had got a job assisting Mrs Parker in the general store—after leaving school with deplorable grades—and every night at seven when it closed, Bernard would be waiting to escort her up the street to Primrose Cottage, where she lived with her Aunt Lucy.

That was all a dozen years ago. It had turned out to be the high point of Ruby's life. Events since then had not been kind to her. First, Bernard had abandoned her for Sally. Then she had started going out with the doctor's son, until she had found out that a girl in the next village was pregnant by him. Soon after, she had lost her job in the store. It had been no fault of hers; simply that trade was falling off and Mrs Parker could no longer pay the wages. Since then, Ruby had lived off social security. When her aunt died in the winter of 1973, Ruby was faced with extra payments for the rent—or moving out of Primrose Cottage. She had found it necessary to take on casual work as a domestic help, occasional mornings that she probably didn't mention when she collected her unemployment money. Her hair had reverted to its natural red. She rarely spoke to anyone, and never to Sally.

Was Ruby still so bitter about the past that she couldn't bring herself to return the letter? If she didn't want to speak, she could easily have pushed it through the door and walked away.

Sally got up and went to see if there was anything on the doormat, but there was not. She opened the door to see if the light was on in Primrose Cottage. It was, but she told herself to be reasonable. Ruby might have come home late. Probably she would return the letter in the morning. If she couldn't face bringing it herself, she might well give it to George Halliwell, the postman, and George would know where it belonged.

Bernard was home and reading the paper when Sally got up next morning. She put her hand on his shoulder and kissed him.

"What was that for?"

"Just for you."

"There's something you want to tell me?"

"No."

The post arrived. Sally said, "I'll get it." She hurried to the door and found two bills. Nothing else.

"What were you expecting?" Bernard asked.

"Nothing in particular."

"Want anything from the store? I think I'll take a walk presently and pick up a *Radio Times*."

Sally said quickly, "I can get it."

Bernard said, "I need some fresh air."

She hated herself for her cowardice. She ought to have told him what had happened. He was entitled to hear it from her.

It was practically certain that he would hear it from *someone* in the village. Even if by some miracle he didn't, he still had a right to know that the love letters he had written for her alone had been read in every house in the village. She would have to tell him, but she couldn't face it yet.

She bit her lip as she watched him stroll serenely up the street in his uniform, confident of the respect that was his entitlement. She almost ran after him, but she did not.

She watched him pass Primrose Cottage, and a horrid possibility occurred to her. Had Ruby kept the letter to hand to Bernard himself, out of some embittered notion of revenge? But he went past and on his way. There was no sign of Ruby.

He was back in twenty minutes with the magazine. He smiled at Sally and said, "How about a coffee?"

"Of course. Who did you meet?"

"Only old George. And Mrs Parker, of course. I want to do a spot of gardening before I have my sleep. The weeds are taking over in the front."

The morning passed with agonizing slowness. Bernard worked steadily in the garden, greeting people as they passed. From the window, Sally saw Ruby emerge from the cottage, but she turned in the other direction, probably to do some cleaning for Miss Seddon, who had the big house by the church.

Jonathan was understandably subdued that morning. He lingered in his room, keeping out of his father's way.

"Did you tell Daddy?" he asked Sally over breakfast.

"Not yet."

"Will he have to know?"

"I expect so." She hesitated. "Jonathan, did you post all the letters that you found upstairs? Every single one?"

"Yes." He gave a sniff. "I'm sorry, Mummy."

"You went up and down the street posting them in all the houses?"

"Yes. I thought they were just old letters."

"They were, but you had no right to do it."

At noon, Bernard had lunch and went to get some sleep.

Michael was back from school. "Everyone knows about Jon and the letters."

"I'm sure," said Sally, "but as far as we're concerned, it's finished. Go and tell your brother lunch is ready."

Early in the afternoon, she crossed the street and rang the bell at Primrose Cottage.

Ruby Simmons was definitely back. Sally could hear her moving about inside. But she didn't come to the door.

Sally pressed the bell a second time. And a third. She refused to be ignored. Recovering that letter mattered more to her than some schoolgirlish feud.

She called out, "Ruby, this is Sally Wilding. I want to speak to you. It's important."

There was no response.

"I think you have something that belongs to me. I want it back, please."

She walked around the cottage to the back door. Before she got there, she heard the bolt drawn across. She stared through the kitchen window. Ruby must have run upstairs.

It was a seventeenth century cottage, and Ruby had not done much to keep it up. Sally could easily have forced a window open and got inside, but that would have been a criminal offence. She came away.

At home, she wrote a note politely asking Ruby to return the letter. She delivered it herself. She heard Ruby come and pick it off the mat. That was all that happened.

That evening, after Bernard had gone back on duty, Sally sat listening for footsteps on the path. Several times, when something in the cottage creaked, she got up to check the letterbox.

She was beginning to feel desperate. She could think of nothing else but recovering that letter. She had tried to shake off the obsession by telling herself that as she planned to destroy the letter anyway, she didn't care about it. But of course she did. She cared for Bernard's sake. And hers. And Jonathan's—that small boy who had given her a lesson in telling the truth.

In bed that night, she thought of a way to get her letter back.

Over breakfast, she said to Bernard, "It's such a lovely morning. Why don't you take Jonathan fishing? You've often promised him, and you said yourself that we should stop treating him as the baby. It will do him good to have an outing with his father."

She watched from the front room window as they went, and she remained there, watching Primrose Cottage.

At about the same time as the previous morning, Ruby came out and turned in the direction of Miss Seddon's.

Sally waited until the street was clear and then crossed to Primrose Cottage and went straight around the side to the back door. It was bolted. She glanced about her. The back windows of the cottage were not overlooked. She took a steel knitting needle from her waistband and pushed it where the wood had warped between one window and the frame.

The catch lifted at the second attempt. She pulled the window open and climbed through.

There were letters on the kitchen table. Hers was not among them. She went into the living room and searched the dresser and the writing-bureau. Drawers, bookshelves, window-sills. Where had Ruby put it?

She went upstairs. A tidy bedroom. The bed made. She spotted the photo at once: a small, framed portrait of Bernard as he had been at seventeen, before he had cut his hair to join the police. Across it, in his handwriting, the words *To Ruby, lots of love, Bernard*. Sally wished she had not seen it.

She went to the dressing table and opened the drawers. She was feeling sick inside. This was the first really bad thing she had done in her life. It was despicable. It was a crime. Yet she had to go on with it.

She started on the chest of drawers. Passed her hand between the layers of clothes. Crossed to the bed and lifted the pillow.

"What are you doing here?"

Sally dropped the pillow and froze.

"What are you doing in my bedroom?" Ruby demanded in a measured voice.

Sally turned. Ruby had the knitting needle in her hand, holding it like a knife. She must have found it by the open window. She must have only gone as far as the store when she went out.

Sally answered with an effort to sound calm, "Looking for my letter."

"It isn't here."

"What have you done with it, then?"

"I haven't got your letter."

"Ruby, I wish I hadn't had to do this, but that letter belongs to me. I want it back."

"And you think that gives you the right to force your way into my home and search my things? That's unlawful entry, Sally Wilding, even if you *are* married to the policeman."

"I'm sorry. If you had opened the door to me yesterday—"

"I didn't wish to. There's no law that says I have to speak to you, but there is a law to protect my home from sneak thieves and intruders, and it's your husband's duty to enforce it. Does he know you're here?"

"No."

There was a moment's pause.

Ruby's mouth twitched. "Get you in a nice spot of trouble if I report this to the police won't it?"

"Don't. Please."

"Why shouldn't I?"

Sally glanced towards the photograph of Bernard.

Ruby said, "You're scum. What are you?"

"Scum."

"Get downstairs. I'll be close behind you."

Sally obeyed. She was humiliated. She didn't know what to expect.

At the foot of the stairs, Ruby said, "Which of your boys was it?"

"Jonathan."

"The little one? How tall is he?"

Sally indicated. "About this high."

"Look at my front door," said Ruby. "See where the letterbox is? My Aunt Lucy had it specially made when the new door was fitted. The kids next door were always playing knock down ginger when they were small, so she had the letterbox as high as possible. Your Jonathan couldn't possibly reach it."

Sally could see that she was right. She should have seen before. She shook her head. She was close to tears. "I don't know what to say."

Ruby said, "Does he know yet?"

"Bernard? No."

There was another pause.

Then Ruby began to laugh. "You poor sap! For the first time in twelve years I wouldn't want to be in your shoes." She opened the door. "Go on, clear off and get what's coming to you."

"Thank you."

"Better take your knitting needle. You may need it."

By the time that Bernard came back from the fishing, Sally had braced herself to tell him everything, but he stopped her. He said, "If this is about those letters, save your breath. I heard it all from Jonathan this morning. That little lad is growing up. He thought it was up to him to put me in the picture. That's worth a lot to me."

"Did he tell you about the letter that hasn't come back?"

"He told me you were still upset. I guessed there had to be a reason."

"You're not too angry?"

"How can I be? It's Friday. I'm off nights."

As they prepared for bed that night, Bernard held up an envelope. "Is this what you were looking for?"

She took it from him. "Yes! Where did you find it?"

"Not a million miles from here. I had another chat with Jonathan. Asked him if he stopped at every house."

"But so did I. He answered that he did. He really did. It just happened that he couldn't reach the letterbox at Primrose Cottage." Sally caught her breath. "He must have pushed it under the door! It was under Ruby's doormat all the time!"

"No. Forget about Ruby. *Every house*, Jon said. That includes this one. He didn't leave us out."

"Here?" Sally frowned. "Jonathan posted one to us? I didn't find it."

"Neither did I."

Her eyes opened wide. "*Michael*?"

"Look at the stamp. That, my darling, was posted on July 1st, 1969, the day Prince Charles was invested as Prince of Wales. The commemorative stamp. It's gold-dust to a stamp collector: a first day cover."

"Michael had it all the time?"

"Picked it off the mat and put it in his album. Most of this time he's been at school. Didn't think we'd miss it. I found the letter in his waste-bin. I don't believe he gave it more than a glance."

She felt herself blush. "I hope not. Bernard, you didn't punish him?"

He shook his head. "As a matter of fact, I promised to look through mine for stamps."

"Your what?"

"My love letters from you."

"You kept the letters I wrote *you*?"

Bernard took her hand. "But I had the foresight to keep mine on *top* of the wardrobe."

LADY IN THE DARK

Victor Canning

FROM THE BUS shelter on the far side of the road he saw the only lighted window of the third floor flat go black. His eyes came down to the swing doors of the entrance to the building. The light came warmly through the entrance to the cold of the thickening dusk.

After a little while a girl passed through the doors and paused at the top of the steps, pulling the thin fur collar of her coat close up about her neck. He watched her come down the steps, turn to the left, and disappear along the darkening road. He had plenty of time. She would be gone for two hours, he knew. He knew so many things. It wasn't difficult to find out all you wanted to know—so long as you were patient and intelligent.

He crossed the road, feeling the wet autumn leaves slip a little under his feet. He passed the main entrance, turned the corner of the building, and went through a side door. Service stairs, guarded with an iron rail, stretched bleakly upwards, grey and institutional under naked bulbs. He climbed to the third floor and with his gloved hands pushed open a small door on the landing. He came out into a chandelier-lit stretch of thickly carpeted corridor.

Away on his right he heard the whine of the lift coming down from the higher floors. He waited until it had passed and then went along to the front door at the far end of the corridor. A brilliantly polished brass plate read *Mrs Walter Courtenay*.

He turned the handle and went in. It was never locked when the maid went out. The old lady didn't like to be locked in. If she rang for the porter she didn't want to have to come and fiddle with a key. Not at her age, not the way she was. He stood just by the door but inside him was a confident feeling of familiarity with the flat. Four months ago the identical flat on the floor below had been vacant. He had looked it over.

He turned and reached up above the door and with a pair of pliers nipped the thin wire of the bell. He hated uniformity of design, but it had its advantages. In all the flats the bell wires ran the same course.

He crossed the little hallway to the door of the sitting room, a room which he knew overlooked the street from which he had watched the flat. But it was not in this room that the light had gone out. That had been in the maid's room to the left. He went in boldly, closing the door firmly behind him.

At once a voice said, "Who is that?" It was the first time he had heard her voice and it was much as he had expected, thin, fragile—like herself, for she must be over eighty—yet with a touch of authority, that pervading tone which he hated, because he would never have it, of culture, wealth, and of easy times and rich places . . . in fact, the whole damned snobbish aristocratic who-are-you-my-man note.

He said, "Never mind who I am. And don't trouble yourself to start ringing bells. I've cut the wires. And don't get alarmed. I'm not going to hurt you."

He went forward and sat down on a chair by the big flat desk. There was a certain amount of light in the room from the street lamps and he could just see her sitting in a stiff chair on the other side of the desk. He could make out the white hair, the erect back, the dull gleam of a cameo brooch at the throat of her dress, and could smell a faintish lavender scent. She had her hands up a little and he saw that she had been knitting when he entered the room.

She said, "It's a most extraordinary introduction. What do you want?"

"I want the key to your safe."

"And a most impertinent demand."

He stirred in his chair, feeling the anger in him rise. The thing was now so nearly over and done with that he was impatient. You got impatient if you lived for a thing for years, got easily angry in front of this kind of talk.

"I said I wouldn't hurt you. I won't. I just want your key. Your maid's out for two hours. You can't ring for the porter. There's nothing you can do."

She moved forward a little in her chair and put her knitting down on the desk. But he noticed, even in the gloom, that one hand still played nervously with a long knitting needle. She might seem in control of herself, but she was nervous all right. That suited him.

"I understand. And when you have the key, I presume you will take my jewels?"

"That's right." He laughed. "They add up to a good life for me from now on."

"So you have not had a good life—as you call it—up to now?"

"I'll say I haven't."

"I see . . . you are that kind of young man."

"How do you know I'm a young man?"

She shook her head gently and her hand tapped nervously on the desk blotter. "I have been blind for twenty years, but that only makes it easier to tell some things. You have a young man's voice. You carry a great load of resentment with you, too. You feel that you have been denied privileges, but you are a fool to imagine that this is the way to right such things."

"Just give me the key. You can tell the police later that your jewels were taken by an under-privileged young man who never went to a decent school. It'll be a great help to them in picking me out from about ten million others."

He pulled a case from his pocket and lit himself a cigarette. For a moment the flare of his lighter showed up the old lady's face, a small, delicate, withered face, like some pale fruit. "I want that key. If you won't give it to me, I shall take it from the chain you wear about your neck."

"Listen to me, young man—" momentarily anger livened the frail voice at the suggestion of such an assault, and she tapped with her knitting needle at the desk, calling him to order—"I have no intention of giving you the key. What is more, I advise you to leave at once. I can give the police a much better description of you than you imagine. But if you go now I will forget this unpleasant interlude.".

"You don't frighten me, and I've wasted enough time. The key!"

"Once more, for your own good, young man, listen to me. Go away at once. Go away and work for the things you want.

Do you think because I am blind that I am helpless? Of course I'm not! I know already a great deal about you which would help the police if you took my jewels. A young man, about five feet ten—voices come from different levels, you know—and wearing a bowler hat, but probably not carrying an umbrella because you wear a raincoat. I can hear it crackle as you move. And I am glad to know that you had the courtesy to take your hat off when you came into this room. Also the grace to be nervous—for you are constantly tapping at the top of your bowler hat as you hold it on your knee. And from the tap I am fairly sure that you are wearing gloves. Also you smoke—without my permission—some kind of American cigarette. It is certainly not English."

He laughed contemptuously. "It's still a description which would fit thousands and thousands in this country. Why should you worry about your jewels? You've got plenty of money. But I haven't. I'm going to have a taste of the things you've enjoyed all your life."

The old lady was silent for a moment, and then she said quietly. "You would take my jewels because they mean money. I never regard them that way. To me, they are memories. They all mean something in my life. If you think I am handing you the key to my safe so that you can walk out of here with my memories you are mistaken."

He stood up, anger spurting in him now. "You're a stupid old woman. What do I care about your memories, about your past? Each jewel a memory!" He laughed harshly. "Well, I'll tell you what I think of your memories. Your husband's photograph in the gold and emerald locket. The lock of hair from your child in the back of the diamond brooch—memories are worth nothing to me. Jewels mean money. Just that for me."

As he moved to go round the desk, her head came up from the position of relapse into which it had sunk at his outburst. Her hands shook with a rapid, indignant movement, and she said vigorously, "Don't dare to come near me! Don't dare, you monster!"

"Then give me the key!"

"You fool—you stupid fool! Go away!"

But he did not go away. He moved slowly round the desk

and stood at her side. If it had to be this way, it had to be. He had come too far, dreamt too long of this, to back away now. Even so, there was something in him which hesitated at the thought of using force on such an old woman.

He paused at the side of the desk, seeing her pale oval face dimly through the gloom of the room as she turned in her seat to face him, and he said, "Come on, the key. You've got no choice." He nipped out his cigarette with gloved fingers and put the stub in his pocket carefully.

But she shook her head. "I will do nothing to help you. Nothing."

He lost his temper then. He stepped towards her, reached out, and grabbed her by the shoulder, feeling the frailness of her body under his hands. She jabbed at his hand with her knitting needle and he caught at her wrists with one hand and held her. Swearing to himself as she squirmed and wriggled, his free hand went to her neck, searching for the chain. He jerked it free, tossed it into the palm of his hand and felt the shape of the safe key.

It was then that he heard her groan and felt her body slump back from him, pulling at the hand with which he held her wrists. She collapsed limply into her chair and he let her wrists go. She made no move.

He stood there for a moment, undecided. She was an old lady. He didn't want it to be true. He had never meant it this way. It couldn't be true. In a few moments she would recover. He went over to the wall and found the picture that covered the safe. It couldn't be true. She would have come round by the time he had collected what he wanted. Nothing could be allowed to stop him now. Not after all the weeks of patient work . . . listening to her maid talking to her boyfriend in the saloon bar three miles from here where she went on her night off . . . his back to them, his ears wide. The safe behind the picture, the chain with the key about her neck. All the work and patience.

He piled the jewel cases into the pockets of his raincoat and when the safe was empty he went back to the old lady. He put his hand on her heart, felt her pulse. It was true. It *was* true! She was gone. Shock. Excitement.

Well, what did it matter? He had what he wanted. Perhaps

it was just as well it was like this—she couldn't even tell the police the few pathetic scraps she had gleaned about him.

At ten o'clock the next morning Detective Inspector Burrows walked into the small but high-class jeweller's shop of Albert Munster and Son to keep an appointment he had made earlier over the telephone with the manager.

Alone with the manager in his office, Burrows said, "I believe a Mrs Walter Courtenay was a customer of yours?"

"That is so. Once every two years her jewellery came here to be cleaned."

"How many people in this shop would handle the stuff?"

"There are only three of us here—myself, my assistant, and the man we have in the workshop who does the actual cleaning."

Burrows looked across at the manager. He was very short, fat, and well over sixty. He said, "I don't think you fit the bill."

"What bill, Inspector?"

"Of the person who last night robbed Mrs Courtenay of her jewels. She was found dead by her maid."

"Dead! How terrible. Poor Mrs Courtenay. But—but, Inspector, what has this to do with us?"

"You'll see." Burrows fished a piece of paper from his pocket. "What I want is a young man, not a public school type, height about five ten, smokes American cigarettes, wears a bowler and a raincoat. What about your workshop man?"

"He's as old as I am. And takes snuff. The description fits young Grierson. But he's not a bad young chap. He's been with me for eight years." He shook his head. "Good lord— Mrs Courtenay dead. I can't believe it."

"It's true enough."

"But what makes you think it's young Grierson?"

"She lived alone with her maid. Never wore the jewels since she went blind twenty years ago. Maid had never seen them. They only left the flat once every two years to come here for cleaning. She knew the thief came from your shop."

"But how could she have told you? She's dead, you say."

"She was a gallant old lady. Blind, but not helpless. More than a match for your Grierson. He came in to her and, I imagine, there was some talk between them while she refused to hand over the key. And while they talked, unknown to him, she was making notes about him."

Burrows referred to his slip of paper and read, "*Young man. Not gentleman. Bowler hat. Gloves. Raincoat. American cigarettes. Angry. Knows jewel details well. Walter in locket. Edith's hair in brooch. Must be from Munster and Son.*"

Burrows put the paper back in his pocket. "Yes, she was no fool. The room was in darkness. She was blind, but right under his nose she wrote it all down on the nice clean blotter on her desk. She wrote it in dots, sticking the point of her knitting needle into the soft blotting paper. Wrote it in dots, poor lady, just six dots that you can arrange into sixty-three combinations and which can tell you anything a blind person wants to tell you. Braille.

"I think you'd better send for young Grierson. Right under his nose—can you beat it? Tapping away with her knitting needle in the dark!"

THE ALL-BAD HAT

H. R. F. Keating

INSPECTOR GHOTE OF the Bombay C.I.D. was not a frequenter of record shops. But on this occasion he was on an important errand. It was soon to be his son Ved's birthday, and Ghote's wife, Protima, had declared that the one thing the boy really wanted as a present was a record of the title song from the new hit movie *Sant aur Badmash*, the one in which two brothers are separated soon after their birth and one becomes a holyman, a saint, a *sant*, and the other becomes a deepest-dyed villain, a *badmash*. And in the last reel they are reconciled.

But Ghote was not finding it easy to make his purchase. From loudspeakers in all four corners of the smart new shop—he had been told it was the best in Bombay—music was pounding out at maximum volume. His attempts to make anyone behind the counter hear had so far come to nothing.

At last he could stand the frustration no longer. He leant across the glossy counter, seized a young man behind it by the sides of his silk *kurta*, and drew him close.

"Please to stop all this noise," he demanded.

"Noise?" said the young man, or rather *shouted* the young man. "What noise is it?"

"That music. That damn music. Kindly get owner here to turn down volume."

"I am owner," the young man answered. "Sole proprietor, Loafer's Delight Disc Mart."

"Then you must turn down the volume," Ghote shouted. "Now."

"Cool it, man," the young proprietor shouted back. "Be cooling it. That volume's good."

"It is bad. Bad, I tell you. I am thinking it may be offence against the law."

"The law? You are making me laugh, man."

Ghote felt a jet of rage fountain up inside him.

"I am an inspector of police," he shouted.

"That is swinging, man," the proprietor riposted. "And I am the son of the Minister for Home."

"Please to behave," Ghote answered, sharply dismissing such impudence.

But whether the young man would have obeyed this injunction or not was never to be put to the test. Down near the entrance of the long, tunnel-like shop, with its smart new racks of records and tapes and its dazzling posters decorating every wall, someone else was not behaving well.

In fact, two tough-looking men, roughly dressed in contrast to the shop's smart clientèle, were behaving extremely badly.

One of the record racks had already been deliberately knocked over. As the shop's young proprietor reduced the volume of his massive loudspeakers almost to nothing, more as a response to the trouble near the entrance than to Ghote's demand, Ghote was able to hear what one of the newcomers was calling out to the other.

"Hey, Chandra bhai, these stands, see how easy they tip over."

"Yes, yes," the other man, a turbaned Sikh, called back. "And these posters. So nice. But, look, already they are torn."

They were not as he spoke. But two instants later they were torn indeed, ripped right off the walls by the man himself.

"Stop," screamed the young proprietor. "Stop. Those are imported. Two hundred rupees each."

Rip. Rip. Rip. Another six hundred rupees went cascading to the floor.

"All right," Ghote said. "I will deal with those two."

He began making his way purposefully down the length of the narrow shop. But the place was too crowded for him to be able to get anywhere near the two troublemakers before, with cheerful shouts of "Sorry, Mr Loafer" and "Good-bye, Mr Loafer Delight," they had reached the entrance and disappeared among the packed pavements of Mahatma Gandhi Road.

However, Ghote had had plenty of time to study the faces of the two goondas and had hurried back to C.I.D. Headquarters and there gone through the fat, tattered books of criminals in the Records section. It had not taken him long to find the two. The Sikh was one Iqbal Singh and the other was a certain Chandra Chagoo.

"I do not think I would have too much of difficulty to nab the pair of them, sir," Ghote said to Assistant Commissioner of Police Samant a quarter of an hour later.

"You are not even to try, Inspector."

Ghote blinked.

"Not to try, A.C.P. sahib? But already I am knowing the favoured haunts of those two. I can have them behind the bars in no time at all."

"You are not to waste your time."

Ghote stared at the A.C.P. across his wide, semicircular desk with its clutter of telephones, pen sets, and teacups. He really could not believe he had heard what he had.

"But, sir," he pleaded, "if you had seen those two goondas, the way they set about breaking up that place, sir. It was a matter of deliberate destruction at Number One level."

"No doubt, no doubt, Inspector. And you know why they were doing all that?"

"Protection racket, sir. The young fellow who owns the place was telling me afterwards. He had been asked to pay and said he would rely upon the police to protect him. It is a very black mark for us, sir."

"And you know why a pair of goondas like that can get away with doing such things, Inspector?"

"No, sir," Ghote had to answer after thinking hard.

"It is because those two goondas that you were taking such trouble to impress on your memory, Inspector, are no more than small fries only."

"Small fries, sir?"

"Exactly, Inspector. You can nab them if you want, but when they come up before the Magistrate, what would we find?"

Ghote decided to leave the Assistant Commissioner to answer his own question.

"We would find that they are having alibis, Inspector. First-class alibis. Two, three, four seemingly respectable fellows willing to swear that at the time in question our two friends

were not in Bombay even. And a damn fine advocate to back
up the tale."

"But . . . but, A.C.P. sahib, alibis and advocates are costing
very much of money. And those two did not look as if they are
having more than two paisa to rub together."

"Quite right, Inspector."

"But then. . . ."

"But the fellow they are working for has got all the paisa
you could wish for."

"And that is who, A.C.P.?"

"It is Daddyji."

"Daddyji, sir?"

"Yes, Inspector. Other names he has and has. But Daddyji
he is known as always. If you had worked on protection racket
cases before, you would have known."

"Yes, sir. He is running many many such rackets then?"

"Not so many, Inspector."

"But, sir, if he is not running many many, then how is he so
wealthy that he can afford such alibis and advocates?"

"It is because of the kind of places he is specialising in
protecting, Inspector. He likes only the best. Anything that is
particularly fine. Best class places only."

"I see, sir. Yes, that is bad."

"He *is* bad, Inspector. Daddyji *is* bad. He is nothing less
than an all-bad hat."

Until this moment, Ghote had been following the A.C.P.'s
explanation with all dutifulness. But these last words stuck in
his craw. An all-bad hat? All bad? He could not find it in
himself to believe it. And foolishly he ventured to express that
doubt.

"But, sir, no man is altogether . . ."

"What is this, Inspector? You, a police officer. You have
seen plenty of miscreants, I hope. Am I going to hear you tell
me there is no such thing as an all-bad man?"

"But . . ."

Ghote thought better of it.

"No, sir."

"Hmm. Well, I grant that most criminals are not all bad.
They are lacking in the guts to be. But that is not meaning that

there are not all-bad men, and of them all, Inspector, the man by the name of Daddyji is the worst. The worst."

"But, sir. . . ."

"No. Let me tell a thing or two about Daddyji, Inspector. Have you got a father?"

"Sir, everybody is having a father. They may not still be. . . ."

"Good. Well, now, perhaps you may not have had good relations with your father. But nevertheless, you were treating him always with a certain respect, isn't it?"

"Yes, sir."

"Daddyji has a father, Inspector. He used to run the gang that Daddyji now has. A pretty tough chap, also. But then came the day when Daddyji thought it was time that he took over. Do you know where that father is now, Inspector?"

"No, sir."

"Take a walk down to Flora Fountain, Inspector. There you would see a crippled man, propped up against the wall, selling little clay figures that he is making."

"Yes, sir. I am knowing him. Very very popular with tourists, the figures he is making. Most lively objects."

"And damn close to falling under Indian Penal Code, Section 292."

"Obscene books and objects, sir. Yes, sir, I think you are right."

"But it is not those that I am concerned with, Inspector. It is his legs."

"His legs, sir?"

"I suppose you are too busy always looking at those figures. But that man's legs are smashed to pieces, Inspector. And it was his own son who was doing that."

"I see, sir. Yes, a very bad hat."

"No, Inspector. An all-bad hat. An all-bad hat. And much too clever to be nabbed by one inspector only. So, leave him. . . ."

He broke off as one of the phones on his wide desk shrilled out. He picked up the receiver.

"Samant. What is it? Oh. Oh, yes, sir. Yes, Minister sahib. Yes? Yes, your son, Minister sahib. Yes, I see, sir. Yes, yes. Yes, at once. At once, Minister sahib."

Slowly A.C.P. Samant put down the receiver. He gave
Ghote, standing neatly to attention on the far side of his desk,
a slow, assessing look.

"So, Inspector, as I was telling, it is not going to be at all
easy to pull in Daddyji. But we are going to do it. You are
going to do it. He has a place down in Colaba. Go over there
ek dum and get out of him something. Something to have him
fairly and squarely on a first-class foolproof charge."

So, scarcely half an hour later, Ghote was standing face to face
with the man A.C.P. Samant had pronounced to be all bad.

Certainly, he thought—looking at the burly frame, the
almost bald bullet head with the thick knife scar running above
the left eyebrow, and the expression of sullen coldness in the
deep-set eyes—the fellow has all the appearance of somebody
who is bad. Very bad even. But all bad?

In spite of everything the A.C.P. had said, Ghote kept his
reservations.

"Well," he said, "so you are the famous Daddyji I have
heard and read a lot about. But you are not so big as I was
expecting. You are not much taller than myself."

"But twice as hard," said Daddyji, his voice grinding out.

"Perhaps. But let me tell you something. However hard or
not hard I am, the C.I.D. itself is harder than you, Daddyji.
Than you or anyone—than any man with a man's weaknesses."

"But I am here. And this is not Thana Gaol."

"No, it is not. But the day for Thana Gaol is coming."

"All kinds of days are coming. The day when elephants are
flying, the day when the sea is drying up. But still I am able to
do what I want."

"But perhaps that time is going to end sooner than you
think. I have a feeling that now you have gone too far."

"I go where I like. Where do you think is too far, my little
inspector?"

"I think," Ghote said slowly, "the Loafer's Delight Disc
Mart was too far. The owner is the son of the Minister for
Home."

But his threat, if threat it was, received only a roar of
uninhibited laughter from the gang boss.

"Oh," he said, wiping his eyes, "that I was not knowing."

"Not when you were ordering his shop to be pulled to pieces?" Ghote slipped in.

But his ruse was by no means clever enough.

"I order, Inspectorji?" Daddyji answered blandly. "But why should you be thinking that?"

"Because that is your modus operandi," Ghote replied. "That is the pattern you are always working to, Daddyji. We know very much about you already."

"You know nothing."

"Oh, perhaps not enough to get a conviction today. But no man is perfect, and one day you would make mistake."

"Oh, yes, mistake and mistake I will make. But it will be no matter."

"No matter?"

Daddyji shrugged.

"If I am making mistake," he said, "it would maybe cost me plenty plenty. But plenty plenty I have. So goodbye to catching Daddyji, Inspector."

"Nevertheless," Ghote said, "I require you to answer certain questions."

"Answers cost nothing."

"If they are not true, they will cost you your freedom."

But Daddyji only smiled.

"They will cost me only the price of making them true after, my little inspector," he said. "And lies are cheap enough."

"We shall see. Now, where were you at 3:15 pip emma today?"

"That is easy. I was here. I am always careful to be with friends at such times, and I was talking with a police constable I am knowing."

"At such times?" Ghote leapt in. "Why were you saying 'at such times'?"

Daddyji smiled again.

"At such times? At afternoon times only, Inspector. It is at such times that a man feels sad, and then it is good to talk. Especially with a police constable."

"Very well. Then tell me, when did you last see two men by the names of Iqbal Singh and Chandra Chagoo?"

"Inspector, will you say those names again?"

"You are very well knowing them."

"Inspector, I have never heard of any such persons. Who are they, please?"

"They are the men you instructed to break up the Loafer's Delight Disc Mart."

Daddyji looked Ghote straight in the eye.

"And you would never be able to prove that, Inspector," he said. "You would never be able to prove that we have ever even met."

So Ghote hardly had anything very successful to report. And A.C.P. Samant was not very pleased.

"And I suppose now," he snapped, "you are proposing to sit upon your bottom and say 'no can do'?"

"No, sir," Ghote answered firmly.

"No, sir. No, sir. Then what are you proposing to do, man?"

"Sir, from my examination of the material in Records I have come to the conclusion there is one good line still to take."

"Records. Records. You are all alike. If it is hiding in Records with a good fan blowing down on you in the heat, you are willing to work and to work. But if it is getting out into the hot streets, you are thinking differently."

"But, sir, I am about to go out into the hot . . . into the streets, sir. To interview the owner of the only place so far to have defied Daddyji's goondas, sir. An establishment by the name of the Galerie Sodawaterwala."

"Galerie? Galerie? What sort of a place is that?"

"It is an art gallery, A.C.P. sahib, and also a shop for the sale of curios and other objects."

"Thank you for telling me, Inspector. And I suppose next you are going to inform me that Sodawaterwala is an old Parsi name. But give me credit for knowing a little bit about some things, Inspector."

"Yes, sir. No, sir. Sorry, sir."

"Well, what for are you standing there, man? Get out there to this Sodawaterwala Gallery and talk to the man."

Mr Sodawaterwala seemed well named. He was a meek and mild-looking individual, evidently with all the artistic leanings of the ancient Parsi community fully developed. But he had refused to pay Daddyji's men any protection money. Even after the police guard he had been given, when he had reported the approach first, had eventually been withdrawn.

"And nothing has happened since those men were withdrawn?" Ghote asked him, with surprise.

"Ah, no, Inspector. But, you see, I took certain steps."

"Steps?"

Mr Sodawaterwala heaved a neat little sigh.

"Inspector," he said, "I must confess. I hired goondas of my own."

"Criminal types? But, Mr Sodawaterwala. . . ."

"Yes, yes. But what was I to do? The very day the police guard was withdrawn, I spotted on the far pavement there the very men who had earlier demanded money. But I am glad to say, Inspector, that both the fellows I hired proved to be altogether charming chaps."

"I am glad to hear."

"Yes, yes. Goondas they may have been, but thoroughly willing and dependable fellows, both."

"They may have *been*, Mr Sodawaterwala? Are they then with you no more?"

"No, no. They are here always by day. But by night, I regret to say, I have been unable to find any others as dependable."

"But have you then left the premises unguarded at night?"

Mr Sodawaterwala suddenly smiled with tremendous impishness.

"No, no, no, indeed," he said. "Come this way, Inspector, and I will show you something."

He led Ghote to an upstairs office over the big gallery showroom, throwing open its door with a flourish. And there, sitting on two stools, were what Ghote took to be at first sight a pair of the most villainous looking goondas he had ever met.

But then he stood peering in at the dimly lit room and looked again.

"They are not real?" he asked. "They are dummies only?"

Mr Sodawaterwala giggled in glee.

"Exactly so, Inspector. Exactly so. A ruse I borrowed from my extensive reading of the crime stories of the West. The Saint, Sherlock Holmes, and so forth. There are just such models as deceived the fierce Colonel Moran when Holmes returned from the dead."

"You were making yourself?" Ghote asked, looking more closely at the extremely lifelike heads.

"No, no, my dear sir. I have no talent in that direction. Yet I am inclined to bet that you will never guess who did indeed make these altogether excellent figures."

"One of the artists whose work you are selling?"

"No, no. Not at all, not at all."

"Then I am unable to guess."

"They were made, my dear, sir, by none other than my sweeper boy."

"A sweeper. But. . . ."

"Yes, yes. But how could a sweeper, a boy of the lowest class, have such a talent? You are right to ask. But, Inspector, let it be a lesson to us. Never underestimate the abilities and complexity of any human being whatsoever."

"He made them by himself, without any assistance?" Ghote asked, looking again at the uncannily lifelike models, still only half able to believe that someone young and untutored could possess such ability.

"Something like a miracle, is it not?" the dapper little Parsi gallery owner said. "And, more than this, the boy—he is about sixteen years of age only—came to me like a miracle."

"How was that?" Ghote asked.

"Well, one morning a few weeks ago my old sweeper, who had been with me for years, announced suddenly that he was leaving. I offered him an increment. I offered him a better place to sleep. He had the use of this cupboard here under the stair. Look."

Mr Sodawaterwala led Ghote to a small door under the stairs and opened it with a flourish.

"You will meet my miracle. . . ." he began.

Then his voice came to an abrupt halt.

"But . . . but this is extraordinary," he said.

"What is it?" Ghote asked, alerted by the note of bewilderment in the Parsi's tone.

"The boy, Piloo. He has gone. Look. All his few possessions, they are here no more. And his pictures. His pictures have gone."

"What pictures are these?" Ghote asked.

"I was telling you, Inspector. Piloo came to me asking for a job just the very day that my old sweeper left so unaccountably. But quite soon I discovered that Piloo was a remarkable artist. He began to play with some scraps of modelling clay that were lying about, and he made these really excellent small pictures. Scenes of everyday life, modelled in clay. I was going to put them on display even."

"He knew this?"

"Yes, yes. Only three days ago I told him. And now he has gone. Vanished. And I really believe he would have become the Indian Hogarth."

Ghote stood in silent tribute for a moment to this odd event in the gallery owner's life. But he could not waste more time.

"Mr Sodawaterwala," he said, "when I saw those dummies of your goonda guards, an idea came into my head. Can I ask you tonight not to put them in their usual place?"

Mr Sodawaterwala visibly paled.

"But, Inspector," he said, "in that case I very much fear I shall be visited by those fellows who threatened me. They will break up the gallery, perhaps even attack me, myself."

"That they should come into the gallery is my object," Ghote answered. "But do not take away the dummies till a late hour. Say, after midnight. Before then I will come and conceal myself on the premises."

"And catch the fellows red-handed?" Mr Sodawaterwala brightened.

"More than that I am hoping," Ghote said. "I hope to catch them and to get them to admit who sent them."

"You think you can do that, Inspector?"

"I think I must do it, Mr Sodawaterwala."

Ghote's mind was still filled with that determination as, just after eleven that night, he cautiously approached the darkened Galerie Sodawaterwala from the rear, the key to its back door, which Mr Sodawaterwala had given him, in his hand.

But he found the little door in the narrow dark lane already unlocked. Worse, forced open.

With pounding heart, he pushed into the echoing empty premises, flashing his pocket torch here and there. All seemed to be well. Nowhere was there any sign of the damage Daddyji's men were likely to have inflicted.

But then, from somewhere up above, he thought he detected a sound. A muffled groan.

He swung the flashlight beam round, located the stairs, pounded up them. Pausing for a moment at the top, he listened. And, yes, distinctly, another groan.

He ran forward.

Mr Sodawaterwala was lying on the floor in the middle of his little upstairs office. His face was black and bloodied. One of his legs was twisted under him at an angle that it should never have been. Both his hands were a mess of open wounds.

Ghote knelt beside him.

"Mr Sodawaterwala," he said, "I am here. I will fetch help. Do not try to move. Where is your telephone?"

"In gallery," the battered Parsi managed. "Down. . . ."

"Yes, yes. Downstairs. I am going. Lie back. Help will be here in a few minutes only."

And, indeed, an ambulance arrived in answer to Ghote's urgent call in a commendably short time. But the interval had been long enough for Mr Sodawaterwala to groan out to Ghote the details of what had happened.

"Daddyji" was the first word that he managed to mutter.

"Daddyji?" Ghote asked. "Did he come himself? Was it him who did this to you?"

"He took pleasure . . . in telling . . . telling me."

Ghote felt a renewed sense of angry determination.

"Then we shall get him," he said. "I am promising you that, Mr Sodawaterwala. But how was it that he knew this was a time to come? Were those dummies still in place?"

"Yes. Yes. Still there. As instructed. But Piloo. Piloo had gone."

"Piloo? Your sweeper boy who disappeared this afternoon? What had he to do with this?"

"Brother."

"Brother? I do not understand."

"Piloo Daddyji's young brother. Daddyji told me. Told me made my old sweeper leave, put the boy in instead. Spy."

Ghote, kneeling beside the broken body of the Parsi, whom he had not liked to move, thought for a little.

"But did you not tell it was some weeks since the boy

came?" he asked at last. "He had time to make the dummies, and for you to discover he was the Indian Garth-ho."

"Hogarth. Hogarth. Very famous British artist. Scenes of low life."

"I am sorry. Hogarth. Yes, Hogarth. But why, if he was sent as a spy, did he not tell Daddyji long ago that you were not really guarded?"

"Because I had told him what a talent he had. He refused for a time to tell his brother."

"Daddyji told you this?"

"Boasted. Said he was giving me extra because . . . because of that."

"Yes, that is very like the man," Ghote said grimly. "But now we would nab him. With your assistance we would do it."

"No," groaned the battered man on the floor beside him.

"But . . . but. . . . No, lie back, Mr Sodawaterwala."

"Inspector, I will not give evidence against that man."

"But, Mr Sodawaterwala, this is the one good chance we have. A man of your reputation, a stainless witness against that man."

"Inspector. Not what I thought I was. Not a fighter for good through and through. Insp. . . . He told me what he would do to me next time."

So it was with feelings of deep pessimism that Ghote reported next day to A.C.P. Samant.

"Sir, Mr Sodawaterwala is recovering well in J.J. Hospital. But he is adamant, sir. He will not give evidence."

The A.C.P. grunted noncommittally.

"And you say this boy, this Piloo, is Daddyji's younger brother?"

"Yes, sir. But if you are thinking that here is a way into that man's heart, I do not. . . ."

"Heart? Heart? I tell you, Inspector, that sort of talk does not apply in the case of Daddyji. He is an all-bad hat. Understand that."

"Yes, sir."

"But the boy took away from the gallery these paintings or pictures or whatever?"

"Pictures in clay, sir. Mr Sodawaterwala believes they will make him the Indian Garth . . . the Indian Hogarth, sir."

"I dare say. I dare say. But the point is that the clay was undoubtedly the property of Mr Sodawaterwala. So the boy stole it. And we are going to put him behind the bars for that."

Ghote felt puzzled.

"But, sir, he was not anything to do with the raid on the Minister's son's record shop, sir."

"But is the Minister to know that, Ghote? Is he? Is he? No, no, we tell Minister sahib that the boy was one of the two brothers and that it has been convenient to bring a charge against one only, and we assure him that the culprit will catch a damn long term of Rigorous Imprisonment. That will get the Minister off our back. And that, after all, is the object of the exercise."

"But, sir," Ghote said, flooded with sudden dismay. "Sir, the boy is the Indian Hogarth. If he is sent to prison, India will lose her Hogarth."

A.C.P Samant brought his fist crashing down onto his desk till every brass paperweight there jumped in the air.

"Inspector," he stormed, "unless you get down to Colaba and arrest that boy now, India will lose her Inspector Ghote."

Less than an hour later, Ghote was once again facing the formidable figure of Daddyji. A smiling, contemptuous Daddyji.

"I had a feeling that I would be seeing you soon, my little inspector."

"I expect so," Ghote returned levelly. "But I have not come to hear where you were at 11 pip emma last night."

That did get home to the iron-tough crook.

"Not? Not? But you must want to know. I was far away. Out at Juhu Beach. With my friends Mahesh Khandwalla, Sudhakar Dalvi, Mohamed Hai, Sudhir. . . ."

"Stop. However many names you are giving, I know you were at the Galerie Sodawaterwala committing grievous bodily harm."

Daddyji brightened at this. Here was a game where he knew the score.

"And you have witnesses?" he asked. "As many as I have?"

"I have one witness. The best. I have the man you beat up."

"And he will give evidence, is it?"

"Why would he not?"

Daddyji shrugged. Elaborately.

"How should I be knowing, my little inspector, why this witness of yours will not tell the lies you are wanting? Perhaps it is that he is afraid."

"Afraid of worse treatment from you," Ghote stated blankly.

Daddyji looked back at him. He held out his wrists as if for handcuffs.

"You are going to arrest me for that then?" he asked.

"No," Ghote said. "Not you, Daddyji."

Again he surprised the gang boss.

"Not me? Then who?"

"I have come to arrest your brother, Piloo."

"Piloo? But you cannot do that. Why, my witnesses will be speaking the truth for him."

"Not when the charge is taking away feloniously from the Galerie Sodawaterwala a quantity of art material—namely, six pictures in clay."

Daddyji relaxed visibly.

"Oh, but take, Inspector," he said. "Take the boy, take."

"Take?"

"Yes. Take, take. For some pieces of mud only, he puts himself in danger. Why should I bother with him?"

"But he is your brother."

"Brother, smother. What is brother? He is one of my men. Or until now he was."

Ghote looked at the broad-shouldered crook.

"Perhaps I should warn you," he said, "the boy is likely to get a long sentence. When someone as influential as the Minister has been insulted by him."

"He can go to gaol for all his life. What am I caring?"

"But his pictures," Ghote said.

"Those things. Pah!"

"But do you not know," Ghote continued earnestly, "that the boy has very, very great gifts. Mr Sodawaterwala says he will be the Indian Hogarth. Hogarth is a very, very famous English artist."

"What is that to me? Here, you will be wanting your

evidence, Inspector. Look under that charpoy there. That is where the boy put his bundle. You will find your pictures there."

Ghote went and knelt beside the rope-slung bed, as much to hide his sense of disgust at Daddyji's behaviour as to get hold of the pictures. They were there, sure enough, and he dragged out the bundle and opened it up, thinking all the while, *Yes, the A.C.P. was right. Daddyji is an all-bad man. All-bad.*

"Hey!"

Daddyji's voice came loudly from over Ghote's shoulder.

"Hey, look at that. It is me. Just as I am. It is me playing cards with Iqbal Singh and that idiot Chandra Chagoo. See, he is losing as always. It is on his face. Wonderful, wonderful."

Ghote looked more closely at the six hard-baked clay tablets. It was certainly true. Small though they were, it was clear beyond doubt that one of the card players was Daddyji, and that on the miniature face of the man the gang boss had pointed out there was an expression of stupid chagrin, as if indeed he was losing at the game and could not understand why.

"Inspector?" Daddyji said, with a note of sudden calculation in his voice.

"What is it?"

"Inspector, I am going to ask you to do something for me."

"For you? You dare to ask?"

Ghote thought with rising anger of how this man was truly all bad.

"Inspector," Daddyji continued, oblivious of Ghote's plain opposition, "I am asking you to take these pictures now to Mr Sodawaterwala and to tell him that, of course, Piloo did not steal them. That he brought them here to show to me only. To me, his brother who had raised him from a boy."

"Take the pictures back? To Mr Sodawaterwala?"

Ghote felt deeply dismayed.

"Then there would be no charge against Piloo," he said.

"That is right," Daddyji answered cheerfully. "And Piloo can go on and make more and more very good pictures like this. He can become the Indian Highlife."

"Hogarth. Hogarth. But. . . ."

And then an idea came to Ghote, an idea so good it was almost incredible.

"You are quite sure you are wanting me to take back these pictures?" he asked, trying to keep his voice neutral.

"But, yes, yes, yes. It is important for Piloo to have this chance. I may be a bad man, Inspector, but I am not all bad. I have some heart left for the boy."

Quickly, Ghote gathered up the little clay tablets, wrapped them, and took them off.

He took them to Mr Sodawaterwala in his bed at the J.J. Hospital.

"And, if what Daddyji told me is true," he said after he had handed them over, "when you get back to your gallery you would find Piloo already back there, making more pictures like these."

Mr Sodawaterwala smiled through his bruised and battered face. A smile of great gentleness.

"But that is wonderful, Inspector," he said. "Wonderful. And Daddyji himself insisted that you have the pictures? It is yet more wonderful. It restores my faith in humanity."

"Yes," Ghote said, "it would seem that my own belief was all the time right. There is no such thing as the all-bad man. Even Daddyji has in him some spark of goodness. You know that his father, Piloo's father, too, has a gift for modelling clay. He is making little, somewhat obscene figures to sell to tourists at Flora Fountain. So the strain of the artist comes to the surface if only in appreciation of what is good, even in a fellow like Daddyji."

Mr Sodawaterwala smiled again.

"But in Piloo," he said, "that strain has gone to the heights. Do you know what I will do for him?"

"It would be something good I am sure."

"I hope so. I am going to hold a first-class, Number One exhibition for him. And, just as soon as I can, I will go back and put these first six pictures of his in the window of the Galerie, as a foretaste."

"Very good, Mr Sodawaterwala. Very good. And I will see that night and day there are four-five hefty constables guarding that window."

"Guarding?" said Mr Sodawaterwala. "But surely, Inspector, now that Daddyji has shown he is not all bad, there is no need for that."

"But there is need, very much of need," Ghote replied. "You see, one of those pictures is very important evidence."

"Evidence? But there is no longer a question of Piloo having stolen any clay. That is ridiculous."

"That is ridiculous, yes. But I will tell you what is not ridiculous: a charge against Daddyji of conspiring with two individuals, namely Iqbal Singh and Chandra Chagoo, to cause damage at the Loafer's Delight Disc Mart."

Mr Sodawaterwala looked bewildered.

"But I do not understand," he said. "How can one of Piloo's pictures have anything to do with such a place as the Loafer's Delight Disc Mart?"

"Because that picture shows Daddyji was a close acquaintance of those two men, something that up to now he was prepared to manufacture evidence to disprove. One of those pictures shows the three of them playing cards together, clearly as clearly."

"Then you are going to arrest Daddyji?" Mr Sodawaterwala asked. "But you cannot do that now."

Ghote looked down at him on the smooth white pillow of the hospital bed.

He sighed.

"Yes, Mr Sodawaterwala," he said, "I can arrest him, and I will. Did you think I can let him go scot-free just because he gave Piloo his chance in life? Yes, even though it was in giving Piloo that chance that he betrayed himself, I must arrest him nevertheless. All bad or partly good, it is my duty to put him behind the bars, and I will do it."

FLIGHT FROM DANGER

Andrew Garve

LARRY SETON WATCHED the two men come up through the trapdoor. The thin one came first, warily, with the flick knife open and pointing. When he was clear the other followed.

The big man lowered the trapdoor, holding it with his foot while he made a looped handle with twine from a spool he'd brought. The old handle had pulled out, leaving a hole, and the last time they'd come up they'd had trouble raising the lid from above once it was shut.

The thin man crossed to Larry and gave him a piece of paper, a grubby envelope and a ballpoint pen. "Okay, write," he said.

Larry wrote as instructed:

Dear Father,

I'm sending you this note so you'll know that what the men said on the telephone was true. They're keeping me locked up in a room where no one ever comes. They say they'll kill me if they don't get the £50,000 and I think they mean it. They are going to ring you again at ten o'clock tomorrow evening. please do as they say about the money and don't try to bring the police in. I'm in good health but rather scared. One of them has a knife. I hope I shall see you again.

Larry

He addressed the envelope and handed it back with the note and the pen. The thin man read the note and gave a satisfied grunt. The big man raised the trapdoor with the loop he'd improvized and the two of them backed down. "You'll soon be

okay now, mate," the thin man called, as he closed the trap
and shot the bolt.

Larry doubted it. Not that he thought his father wouldn't pay
the money. The old man was rich, and he'd take the one
chance that offered, however slender it seemed. He'd hope
that the kidnappers would be as good as their word and let
Larry go when the money was paid. But Larry knew they
wouldn't. They couldn't afford to—because he knew who they
were, and they knew he knew. He'd seen them at his father's
factory, where they'd been working as building labourers on a
plant extension until a week or two ago. He didn't know their
names, but if he ever got free again he'd be able to tell the
police enough to make a capture pretty certain. So he wouldn't
be allowed to go free. Once they'd got the money, they'd kill
him. Larry had read the intention in the thin man's vicious
little eyes.

He gazed desperately around his prison. It was a bare loft,
about twelve feet by twenty, poorly lit and black with grime. It
had no exit but the trapdoor, and no windows. The sloping
raftered sides met in a square of flat roof with a skylight in it
that had lost its glass—but the skylight was ten feet up and
barred with iron bars. There was no way of escape.

No chance, either, of making a fight of it—not a successful
one. Larry was sixteen and pretty well set-up—but you couldn't
argue with a knife. *He* couldn't, anyway. And the kidnappers
always came up together. They gave him no chances. It would
be different if he had some weapon. But there wasn't anything
in the loft that would serve him. A few bits of glass on the
damp boards beneath the skylight—but too small to be of any
use against a knife. A wooden orange box that they'd brought
up to serve as a writing table—too unwieldy to make much of
a weapon. Apart from that, they'd left him with almost nothing.
A plastic beaker and a plastic water container. A plastic
bucket. A plastic plate which still held the remnants of his
supper. A few wax candles for use at night. The spool of twine
that the big man had chucked into a corner after fixing the lid.
And that, literally, was all.

For a moment, Larry concentrated on the new object, the
spool. It was a big spool, machine-rolled, and the twine was

strong. Could he use it? Fantastic ideas chased each other
through his head. Rig up a trip line? Weave it into some kind
of net? Garotte one of the men with it? Not very promising
. . . If there'd been a window he might have dangled something
down and tried to attract attention. But there wasn't a window.
Or if the skylight had been lower, he might have tried throwing
the spool through the bars, with a message on it. He wondered
if it was possible. He put the orange box under the skylight,
up-ended, and climbed on to it. It was old and frail and gave
out ominous cracks. Cautiously, he raised his hand. He was
still short of the bars by more than a foot. It would be difficult
to throw the spool through the bars, which were only four
inches apart. And even if he got it through, it would go straight
up and fall straight down again on to the flat roof. No good.
He'd need a rocket to get it away from the roof. . . .

A rocket! No chance of that, of course—but it started a
train of thought. . . . He climbed down and stood considering.
Could he? He gazed up through the skylight. Light clouds
were moving steadily across the evening sky. Quite fast. There
was plenty of wind up there—he could feel the draught through
the opening. He looked around, appraising his resources. The
twine, the bits of glass, the wooden box. The nylon shirt he
was wearing. There was just a chance. Anyway, what had he
got to lose?

He examined the bits of glass. There was a piece with a
sharp edge. That should do. He examined the box. The thin
strips of wood that formed its sides would probably give him
what he needed. It would take time—but he had plenty of
that.

He lit a candle in the failing light and stuck it in his water
beaker. Then he peeled off his shirt and spread it on the
floorboards. There was more than enough material in the shirt
tail, if he made no mistake. He'd better mark it out first. But
with what? He looked about him. Dirt from the floor—and
water? Or from the rafters? He ran a finger along one of them.
It came away coated with soot. There was so much soot that
he could scrape it off into his hand. He made a little pile of it
on the floor, and puddled it, and applied some to a bit of the
shirt with a sliver of wood from the box. The mixture wasn't as
good as ink, but it left a mark. It would do.

Carefully, now, using the box as a straight edge, he sketched his quadrilateral on the nylon. The last time he'd done this was five years ago—but he hadn't forgotten the lore his father had taught him. It wasn't the size that mattered, but the proportions—and those he remembered. The lower sides one and a half times the upper sides. Leave enough material for turning in and sewing. And four flaps for making pockets to hold the struts. . . . That should be all right.

Cutting out the shape was a long job. The nylon was strong and wouldn't tear. The piece of glass wasn't nearly as effective as a knife. The end product was ragged at the edges—but it would serve.

Now for the struts. Pull one of the thin battens from the box. Score down it with the glass, half an inch from the edge. Deeper, now. Then the other side. Now a little pressure. . . . The wood split, and he had his vertical strut. He worked quietly, methodically, intent on the job. The kidnappers had taken his watch and he could only guess at the time. Occasionally he lit a fresh candle from the stump of the old one.

Sewing the edges, and making the pockets for the struts, was another long job. He used a loose nail from the box to make the holes, and twine from the spool to thread through them. He tied the struts where they crossed. Finally, he stood back.

It wasn't much of a kite. A bit of a lash-up. All the same, if he could once get it through the skylight, it should fly. When it was well up, he'd let it go, and it would fall, with the message he was going to write on it. . . .

It was only when he began to think about the message that he realized he'd almost no information to give. He'd no idea where he was. He could remember nothing from the time he'd been knocked out till he'd come round in the loft. He thought he was in a town, because of the distant hum of traffic, but he didn't know if he was still in London. A dirty loft at the top of a building—that was all the description he could give. That wouldn't bring rescue. He could say that his kidnappers had worked at the factory, but that wouldn't bring rescue either—certainly not in time. Anyway, there wouldn't be room on the kite for a long message. With his improvized ink, the letters would have to be large and thick to be legible.

He pondered. There was no point in letting the kite loose

without adequate directions. Better to keep it tethered, and say who'd sent it up. When the wind dropped, it would fall, and someone would find it and follow the string. That was it. . . .

He wrote his message with laborious care. Big letters, well blacked in. FROM LARRY SETON. Every newspaper reader would know that name by now. TELL POLICE. DON'T BREAK STRING. That should do it.

Once more he considered. Assuming the kite flew, how long a scope should he give it. In a way, the shorter the better—it would be quicker and easier for the police to follow the string. But suppose it came down on a roof top—or in a tree? Then it might not be found at all. Better to let it fly high and have some more messages. Spaced along the string. Then, wherever it fell, there'd be a good chance that one of the messages would be seen. He cut out some strips of nylon and wrote the same words on them.

Now he was ready to try the kite. He made the end of the twine fast to it and climbed again on to the orange box. He could just reach to push the kite through the bars. It lay flat on top of them, stirring a little in the wind but not lifting enough to take off. Somehow he'd have to raise it, give it a start. He thought for a moment, then broke another thin batten from the box and set to work to cut it into strips. Three or four strips bound together with twine made a long rod. He climbed back on the box and poked the rod through the bars. At the second attempt he found the kite's balancing point and raised it on the rod. In a moment the wind caught it and it was off, straining at the twine, beautifully steady.

Larry could only guess how much twine he was letting out into the darkness above. At what he thought was about a couple of hundred feet, he tied on one of his strip messages. He let out more twine, and tied on another. Near the end of the string, he tied a third.

Now for tethering the kite. The twine had been wound on a stout cardboard cylinder. Released crosswise under the bars, that would do the trick. Of course, the kidnappers might notice it when they came up in the morning. But they might equally notice that the spool of twine had gone—or that the box had been partly dismantled. The whole thing was a gamble.

With the end of the twine fast to the cylinder, Larry climbed once more on to the box. He would have to stretch his arm to the limit to make sure the cylinder got wedged across the bars. Balanced on the box, he reached for the skylight, straining, the cylinder at his finger tips. . . . Then, without warning, with a sudden splintering crash, the box collapsed under him. As he fell, the cylinder slipped from his grasp. When he looked up from the floor, he saw that it had been drawn through the bars and had disappeared.

He put on the remnants of his shirt, and his jacket, and sank to the boards in despair. With the kite loose, the message he'd written would help no one. FROM LARRY SETON. TELL POLICE. DON'T BREAK STRING. Nobody would find him on that information. His efforts had all been in vain.

2

Superintendent Grant, in charge of the Seton kidnapping case, was in his office with Larry Seton's father. He had just seen the letter that had arrived from Larry that morning. Now he and Seton were discussing what action to take. Seton, grey with anxiety and sleeplessness, wanted to pay up and keep the police out of it. Grant wanted to set a trap. They were still arguing when Sergeant Ellis entered.

"This has just been brought in, sir. Found in North London—Primrose Hill." He put a kite on the table. There was a short length of twine, about twenty feet, attached to it, with a frayed end where it had snapped.

Grant read the message, fingered the black lettering, examined the fabric. "Could be another hoax," he said doubtfully. He'd already been led off on one false scent.

Seton shook his head. "It's genuine—I'm sure of it." His voice had an edge of excitement. "Larry and I used to make kites like this when he was a lad. We were pretty expert—and he's remembered the model. The proportions are the same. The shape's right. I'm as sure as if he'd put his signature to it that he made it."

"I see." Grant grew brisk. "Where exactly was it found, Sergeant?"

"Hanging down over a window at number 12, Lucy Street. Chap in a bedsitter there—name of Forbes—found it this morning and dropped it in at his local station on his way to work."

"We might be able to find the rest of the string and trace it back," Seton said eagerly. "We might find him. . . ."

Grant nodded. "Let's go."

The superintendent studied the upper part of Number 12, Lucy Street, through binoculars. Presently he gave a grunt. "I can see it. It's hanging from the gutter—looks as though it goes over the top of the house. Let's try the next street."

They drove round and quickly picked up the trail again. From the house the string crossed the street at rooftop level. With many detours, they continued to follow its course. In several places it was broken and they had to cast around for the next piece. Twice they were helped by the sight of bits of white material attached to it. They traced it over buildings; over the branches of a tree; across a big coal yard; between two linked coal trucks on a rusty line; past a group of men preparing to unload the foremost truck; on over a factory roof. Then, when hope was rising fast, they came upon a cardboard cylinder hanging from a lamp standard, with broken twine attached. Beyond, there was nothing.

"Larry must have let it go," Seton said, in a tone of deep dejection.

Grant nodded. "Maybe he was interrupted before he could make it fast. Bad luck. Still, we've got something to work on." He returned to the police car and radioed some instructions.

It took a squad of policemen and a fire brigade detachment more than two hours to collect up all the bits of string they could find. Each one had to be numbered and labelled and its exact position marked on a street plan before removal. There were eight breaks, all of them at street crossings—caused, no doubt, by passing traffic.

Back at the Yard, Grant had the bits of string put together and measured. Allowing for the street gaps where sections had been carried away, the total length was almost two thousand feet. The recovery data, now plotted on a big wall plan, showed that it had flown, with much bunching and many twists and turns, in a roughly northerly direction from Lucy Street. To the point where they'd found the cardboard cylinder, the beeline distance was 1200 feet. Somewhere beyond that, perhaps a long way beyond, was Larry.

Grant said, "You're the expert, Mr Seton. What would you expect to happen to a kite flying on a 2000 foot string when the end was released?"

Seton shook his head. "It's hard to say. Every kite behaves differently. The strength and consistency of the wind would clearly be a big factor. The weight of the string would be another. In general, if there was a good wind I'd expect the kite to shoot up rapidly for a short distance, lifting the string with it. Then it would begin to fall, fluttering down, diving and looping, making a good deal of leeway with the wind and carrying the string with it. To find out what this kite did, one would have to fly it experimentally in exactly the same conditions—and that's obviously impossible."

"We don't even know when the kite was released," Ellis said.

Grant frowned. "What time was it found?"

"One o'clock this morning, sir. That was the time Forbes arrived home from a party. He got into bed and then he heard a tapping on the window. It annoyed him, so he went to see what was causing it, found the kite dangling, and yanked it in. He didn't put on a light so he didn't see what was written on it till this morning. . . . Anyway, he was sure it was one o'clock when he found it."

"Then just before one o'clock is the latest time it could have been released," Grant said. "Now what about the earliest time?"

"Well, Forbes said it wasn't there when he left for work yesterday morning, or he'd have seen it dangling."

"So it was released some time between, say, eight o'clock yesterday morning and one o'clock this morning. Seventeen hours . . . I wonder if the Met. people can help us."

Grant was on the phone for some time, making notes as the Met. men talked. His expression grew gloomier as he wrote.

"Not much help, I'm afraid," he said, as he hung up. "What you might call typical English weather. The wind yesterday morning was southwesterly, force five. In the afternoon it veered through northwest to north, dropping to force three. At night a narrow ridge of high pressure crossed London and the wind was northeasterly, force two at first, increasing to force three. Then in the early morning it backed again to northwesterly, force two."

"So we're no further forward," Seton said. "The kite was obviously released when the wind was in the northern quadrant—but which bit of the quadrant, and at what force?"

"If only there was some way of narrowing down the time," Grant said. He sat silent for a while. Then a speculative look crept into his face. "Those coal trucks that were being unloaded—I wonder. . . ." Once more he reached for the telephone.

This time, when he hung up, his expression was jubilant. "A long shot—but it worked. Those two coal trucks were shunted in just after ten o'clock last night—and the string fell between them. So now we know the kite was released between ten o'clock and one. I think I'll have another word with the Met. Office."

He made more notes as he repeated the information for the others to hear. "Ridge of high pressure—yes. Wind northeasterly force three up to 5,000 feet throughout the period. . . . Wind steady, not gusty. . . . Now tell me, is there anywhere where those conditions are being repeated at this moment . . . ? Ridge has moved on—I see . . . Yorkshire . . . What part of Yorkshire . . . ? Anywhere in the East Riding. . . . And for how long. . . . ? About four hours. . . ." Grant glanced at his watch. "Thanks a lot."

He hung up. "Right," he said. "Let's go to Yorkshire and fly a kite."

Just under three hours later, an Army helicopter set down the police party on a disused airfield a few miles inland from the Yorkshire coast. A cool but gentle breeze was blowing steadily from the northeast. The sky was clear.

Grant positioned his men and Seton put the kite up. It rose

quickly and smoothly as the knotted twine was let out. In a few minutes Seton was left with the bare cylinder. For a moment he held on. The kite was almost stationary, a mere dot against the blue to the southwest.

"Right, let her go," Grant said.

Seton released the cylinder. It shot about fifty feet into the air, then drifted away out of sight as the kite hesitated, began to dive, turned and twisted, and slowly fluttered to earth.

A distant watcher signalled where the kite had fallen and police surveyors got to work, checking the distance from release point to impact point, and the direction. Grant noted the results in his book. The kite had fallen 2,250 feet from the point of release, on a magnetic bearing of 215 degrees.

Back at the Yard in the early evening, Grant drew a circle on the wall plan—2,250 feet from number 12, Lucy Street, on the reverse compass bearing.

"Well, that should be it," he said. "Somewhere around there. Now what kind of place are we going to look for?"

"A pretty high building," Seton said. "With some sort of exit to a roof, I should think, or I can't see how Larry could have got the kite up."

"Probably not a private dwelling," Ellis added. "Kidnappers wouldn't risk keeping anyone shut up where there were other people around—particularly after all the publicity there's been. These villains usually hide out in disused premises—empty warehouses, garages, that sort of thing."

Grant nodded. "I was thinking the same. An industrial building of some sort. . . . ? I've just had the lab. report on the substance used for the message on the kite. It's soot. . . . Right, let's go."

The circle, they found, enclosed an area of dingy tenement buildings, a few factories, a scrap metal dump and a surprising amount of waste ground. Only the occasional new housing block relieved the squalor. Grant divided his force into groups, each with a walkie-talkie, and allotted them streets. Every building of the slightest interest was to be reported on and discussed.

Within the circle, they found nothing. Grant widened the

field of search to take in the surrounding streets. It was almost dusk when Ellis suddenly exclaimed, "How about that, sir?"

Grant looked ahead at the building. A blackened sign on the wall said "Oakley Furniture Company. Depository and Repairs." It was a tall building, Victorian Gothic with a kind of tower at one end. As they drew nearer, Grant saw that in fact it was only the skeleton of a building. Fire had gutted it. Warning notices above the corrugated iron fence enclosing the site said "Danger. Keep out." But not everyone had kept out, for two of the corrugated sheets had been forced apart, leaving a two-foot gap.

Cautiously, Grant led the way through the gap. He saw at once that not all the building had been destroyed. At the tower end there was a flight of stone steps, intact. They climbed. Soot lay thickly everywhere. Soot from the fire. Through a broken door on the first landing they saw junk, bits of broken furniture, black and abandoned stores. Tensely, Grant pointed. To a dirty spool of twine. "Used for furniture repairs," he said softly. "This is it."

They came to a closed door. Voices were audible inside. Grant gently tried the door. It opened a fraction. Ellis moved up beside him. "Right," Grant said, and they burst in. Two men were playing cards on the floor by candlelight. They sprang up.

"Okay," Grant said, "take it easy. We're the police. Where is he?"

The man with the vicious little eyes gave an involuntary glance upwards. Seton shouted "Larry!", and made for the ladder.

DEAD GROUND

June Thomson

MAJOR ROSSITER LIKED to think of it as *his* view, partly because no other house in the village shared it but largely because he had bought Charmont Villa for its sake.

The house itself was undistinguished looking. Detached and vaguely neo-Tudor in design, it was built of red brick with diamond-pane windows of such mean proportions that all the rooms were dark and oppressive. It stood in three-quarters of an acre of neglected garden and was, in addition, an inconvenient half a mile from the village.

All these reasons should have dissuaded Major Rossiter from buying it. Indeed, as he had tramped round it with his wife two years earlier, accompanied by the estate agent, his reaction had been that they were wasting their time. He had indicated as much to his wife, shaking his head at her behind the fellow's back. Not that Phoebe would have expressed an opinion. She left that sort of decision to him. And quite right, too.

No, he was looking for something completely different; somewhere pleasant where he could enjoy his retirement from the army; not too much garden; close to a golf club and a decent pub and in the type of area where he would find people to share his interests: a little bridge, the occasional dinner party, a bit of rough shooting.

He doubted if the village would supply any of these. The sight of it as they had driven through on their way to view the house was enough to put him off. It was a dreary little place in the Major's opinion, its centre dominated by a ramshackle garage and a huddle of outbuildings constructed almost entirely, it seemed, out of corrugated iron.

He had commented on it as they passed.

"That needs coming down for a start," he had said, only half jokingly.

That was before he saw the house and decided, as soon as they stepped inside the gloomy hall, that he had no intention of buying the place anyway.

"And this is the lounge," the estate agent had announced, throwing open a door.

Lounge! Good God! Major Rossiter had thought, surveying the pink-flowered wallpaper, the mock parquet lino, the castellated fireplace of bright red bricks.

And then he had seen the view.

Even framed in the two tiny windows which overlooked the back garden and cut into pieces by the fiddly little diamond-panes, it had been—well, impressive was hardly the word.

It was stupendous! Magnificent! Overwhelming!

It extended for miles beyond the shaggy lawn and the overgrown shrubs of the garden; a wide vista of cornfields and pasture running down to water meadows and the river which swept round in great, shining curves, glittering in the afternoon sunshine, before rising on the far side to more open farmland and the distant wooded slopes of the horizon.

Almost as if he had been bewitched, he heard himself saying, "Yes, I'll take it."

He meant the view, of course, not the house. It was only when he saw the look of gratified astonishment on the estate agent's face that he recovered his senses sufficiently to add, "Subject to contract and a satisfactory surveyor's report."

"Are you sure, George?" his wife had asked later as they drove away.

Sure? Of course he was sure. He had never been so certain of anything in his life before.

"Only the kitchen seemed a little. . . ."

"Oh, we'll soon sort that out," Major Rossiter had interrupted her confidently. Indeed, it was rare for Mrs Rossiter ever to finish a sentence. "All it needs is a few new fitments."

But his mind was not really on kitchen cupboards and sink units. He was busy planning much more exciting and important improvements.

He'd have those two tiny windows out for a start and the whole of that back wall demolished to take a huge floor to ceiling picture window which would bring the view into the drawing room. Then the garden would have to be replanned, the lawn extended, those trees which partly obscured the vista cut down and a patio built outside the window. His imagination rested fondly on long summer evenings when, decanter and soda syphon at his side, he would simply sit and gaze at the view. His view!

The house was duly bought and, over the next year, Major Rossiter put his plans into action. Surveying it when everything was finished, the curtains hung, his cups for shooting lined up on the bureau facing the picture window, which now formed a magnificent fourth wall, Major Rossiter felt well pleased with himself. He had come to grips with the damned place.

The garden proved less tractable. The main problem was the field which lay at the bottom, between his property and the view. Once the trees and bushes were removed in order to open up the vista, Major Rossiter discovered to his annoyance that the field was also revealed and could be overlooked from the drawing room window.

It was a small, neglected paddock, dock and nettle ridden, containing a dilapidated stable in one corner in which an old white horse appeared to have taken up residence. Not only did the horse lean over Major Rossiter's fence to observe the house with melancholy interest as it browsed on the shoots of his newly planted rhododendrons, but it was possible to see the corrugated iron roof of its stable no matter how carefully the Major positioned his trees and shrubs.

"If I owned it, I'd pull the blasted thing down," Major Rossiter told his wife.

"Perhaps you could buy the field," Mrs Rossiter suggested mildly at which her husband snorted with derision at the absurdity of the idea before leaving the room and slamming the door behind him.

Buy the field! The woman didn't know what she was talking about. Hadn't he got enough garden to cope with as it was? What would he do with a scrubby little piece of land like that?

However, over the next few days, as Major Rossiter prowled about the garden, shooing away the horse and glaring at the ramshackle shed it occupied, the idea took seed.

Why not buy it? he thought. Land was always valuable and

he could not imagine the owner of the field would ask much for such a miserable bit of it.

Careful inquiries in the village elicited the owner's name and two days later, dressed in tweed hacking jacket and cavalry twill trousers, Major Rossiter's tall, upright figure set off in search of Mr Blower, swinging his walking stick confidently.

Mr Blower was not difficult to find. In addition to the paddock, he owned the run-down garage which dominated the centre of the village.

It was a damned eyesore, Major Rossiter decided, surveying it disapprovingly at close quarters as he approached the fore-court. An ugly, pebble-dashed bungalow, its garden full of broken-down cars and piles of old tyres, occupied one side of the site. The other was taken up by a huge, barn-like construc-tion of creosoted wood where repairs were carried out by Mr Blower and his son, although Major Rossiter, viewing the pair of them in passing, wouldn't have trusted as much as Mrs Rossiter's bicycle to either of them. A small shed, not unlike the one which the horse occupied and which spoiled the Major's view, labelled optimistically "Office", sat in the middle behind the petrol pumps. It was from this building that Mr Blower emerged as Major Rossiter approached.

"Morning, Major Rossiter!" Mr Blower greeted him, although quite how the fellow had acquired his name the Major was at a loss to understand.

He was a small, bright-eyed, slightly bandy-legged man, dressed in filthy overalls, with one of those ingratiating smiles which the Major instinctively distrusted.

"Ah, Blower!" Major Rossiter returned, coming to a halt in front of the petrol pumps. Uncharacteristically, he felt at a loss how to begin. He was not used to doing business with men like Blower; more usually he gave them orders. Consequently, he had not the faintest idea how to address the man; hardly as an equal, but as a superior officer to an other-ranker also seemed inappropriate, despite Blower's oil-stained hands and local accent.

"There's a small—matter of—ah—business I'd like to dis-cuss with you," the Major began.

At the word "business", Blower's face assumed a serious

expression although his eyes continued to twinkle disconcertingly.

"In that case, Major, you'd better step inside," he replied, leading the way into the tiny office. "So what can I do for you?" he continued, leaning up against the desk which was littered with old sparking-plugs.

"Actually, I wanted to see you about that field behind my house which I understand you own," the Major replied in an off-hand voice. "I could be interested in buying it if the price suits me, not that it's going to add much to my property."

Better not sound too eager, he thought. Keep the fellow in suspense.

"Ah, that field," Blower said ruminatively. "Nice bit of land, that."

"In rather poor condition, I'd say," the Major countered. "Full of docks and nettles. I also noticed the fences want repairing."

"You could be right there," Blower conceded magnanimously. "But there's the stable as goes with it. Useful, that. You could store a lot of stuff in there."

"Judging by the state of the roof, I doubt it's weather-proof," Major Rossiter retorted.

"Only needs some bits of corrugated iron tacked on here and there. You could likely pick up a few sheets cheap. As a matter of fact, I've got a fair amount of it knocking about the place here."

"How much?" Major Rossiter demanded.

It was time, he felt, that the preliminary skirmishes were finished and the real negotiations began.

Blower thought, head on one side.

"I reckon I could do the lot for ten quid."

"I mean the field, man!" Major Rossiter exclaimed impatiently. For the first time during the conversation, it occurred to him that Blower was finding a great deal of quiet amusement in the situation.

There was a small silence as Blower regarded him with his bright little eyes.

"Two thousand," he said at last.

"Two thousand!" The Major was scandalised. Drawing him-self up to his full height, he looked the fellow up and down,

from the top of his greasy cap to the toes of his battered boots
which protruded from the torn cuffs of his overalls. "Good
morning, Mr Blower," he continued stiffly. "If you ever consider putting the field on the market at a more acceptable
price, I might be interested in doing business with you," and
he turned away without giving the man a second glance.

As he said later to his wife, "I've put the ball firmly in the
fellow's court. It's up to him now."

But Blower seemed unaware of this fact for, although the
weeks passed, he made no attempt to approach the Major nor
to reopen negotiations. Meanwhile, the horse continued to
occupy the paddock and to browse quietly off the top of the
flowering shrubs as it contemplated the back of Charmont Villa
and its garden. The Major, in his turn, stood at the picture
window glaring much less pacifically at it and the corrugated
iron slope of the stable roof which protruded itself infuriatingly
into the bottom left-hand corner of his view, quite ruining the
magnificent sweep of cornfield and river, meadow and distant
woods.

As day succeeded day and still Blower made no move, the
Major's temper shortened until the sight of the horse and its
stable became so intolerable that he could no longer bear to
stroll about in his own garden.

It was an absurd situation in which to find himself and all
because of that wretched little plot of land.

And then, on Sunday morning, events began to move.
Phoebe, returning from church which she always attended
alone, Major Rossiter having quarrelled with the vicar over
the question of nuclear disarmament, announced that there
was a car parked in the paddock gateway and a man was
measuring the field.

"Blower, d'you mean?" her husband demanded.

"I don't think so, dear," she replied. "He's wearing a suit."

Major Rossiter flung down the newspaper and went to
reconnoitre.

For once, Phoebe was right. The man pacing out the paddock
was not Blower. He was a tall, gangling individual, dressed in
bright navy blue with a broad chalk stripe, and with one of
those heads which, even at a distance, looked common, having

a distinctly underbred slope to the back of it and greasy, dark
hair worn too long at the nape of the neck.

The man seemed absorbed in his task and was unaware
either of the Major's curiosity or the horse's which, banished
to its stable, was watching his actions over the top of the half-
door.

Major Rossiter watched, too.

The man was clearly measuring an area of the field by pacing
slowly and carefully across it, halting every so often to thrust
what appeared to be a small stick in the ground.

But what was he doing in Blower's field? And what was he
measuring? A new stable? It seemed unlikely. Judging by the
distances he covered, it was of largish dimensions; certainly
much bigger than the shed, and appeared to occupy the centre
of the paddock; in other words, the area in a direct line from
the Major's garden and drawing room window.

As Major Rossiter stood watching, the man completed one
side and turned in his direction, at which the Major beat a
hasty retreat, dodging behind the rhododendrons, well out of
the fellow's line of sight.

As a strategic withdrawal, it was briskly executed but still
left the enemy, if he should be considered as such, in pos-
session, literally, of the field; and Major Rossiter, although
uncertain of the man's exact intentions, did not doubt for a
moment that they boded ill for him in the long run.

It was equally obvious that the man's presence in the paddock
was ultimately Blower's responsibility. After all, he owned it.
Remembering Blower's bright little eyes and air of suppressed
amusement, Major Rossiter was quite certain that some form
of skullduggery was going on and that Blower was at the back
of it.

It was a situation which could not be ignored. Despite his
assertion that the ball was in Blower's court, Major Rossiter
had the uncomfortable feeling that at some point during the
past six weeks, when he hadn't been looking, Blower had
lobbed it back at him.

There was only one way to find out: a direct confrontation
with Blower and, on Monday morning, a plan of campaign
carefully worked out in his mind, Major Rossiter drove on to
the garage forecourt where he was served petrol by Blower's

son, Vernon, short of stature like his father but of a sullen rather than a jaunty temperament.

"Fill her up!" the Major told him in a loud, magnanimous voice and, when the tank was full, he followed the young man into the office where he had already noticed Blower senior ensconced at the desk behind the dirty window, drinking tea from an enamel mug and filling in a form with an indelible pencil.

"Ah, Mr Blower!" Major Rossiter exclaimed with cheery surprise as if Blower was the last person he expected to encounter there. "How are things with you?"

"Not bad," Blower replied warily, as if uncertain how to react to the Major's mood. "Mustn't grumble."

"No, indeed we mustn't. After all, it's a beautiful day," the Major returned, waving an expansive hand towards the filthy glass behind which the clear spring sunshine fell on petrol pumps and oil drums, perilous pillars of old tyres and the rotting carcasses of cars.

He broke off as the sullen youth counted out his change, which he pocketed before nodding to the two Blowers and walking to the door where, as if suddenly reminded, he stopped short, his hand on the knob.

"Oh, by the way, Blower, I suppose you've not had any more thoughts about that bit of land, have you?" he inquired casually.

Describing it that way was rather a good ploy, he thought. It struck the right off-hand note, expressing a certain contempt for the property, thus diminishing its worth.

Blower rubbed a hand slowly across his chin.

"Well, now," he said, sounding uncharacteristically embarrassed, "I don't quite know how to put this, Major, but I'm up against a bit of a problem there."

"Oh, really?" Major Rossiter replied.

An innate sense of coming disaster made him refrain from saying any more.

Blower took a deep breath before beginning.

"It's like this. I know you was round here asking about buying that field—when was it, six weeks ago?—and like I said to you at the time, I might be interested if the price was right. . . ."

"Get to the point, man," Major Rossiter interrupted impatiently.

Good God, he was as bad as Phoebe, wittering on.

"Well, the point is, Major, since I spoke to you last, I've had somebody else keen to buy it. . . ."

"The man who was there yesterday measuring up?" Major Rossiter demanded, and immediately regretted having spoken. It had been his firm intention to say nothing about having seen the man; not that Blower took any notice. Having launched into his account, he was not going to be diverted from it.

". . . who's willing to pay the full asking price *and* put down a deposit to show he means business. And that's even before he's sure he'll get planning permission although I can't see him having too much trouble, building land being scarce round here and him with five kids. . . ."

"Planning permission for what?" Major Rossiter raised his voice, cutting across Blower's narrative.

"A four bedroomed house." Blower seemed surprised that the Major was ignorant of this fact. "Double garage. Through lounge. Paddling pool for the kiddies. He's got it all worked out. He did say paddling pool, didn't he, Vernon?" Mr Blower broke off to appeal to his son who was lounging against the till, picking at a filthy hangnail on his right thumb.

"Yeah, that's right," Vernon replied. "And a workshop. Does up racing cars as a hobby."

"There now," Blower said beaming, as if gratified that his statement had been verified.

Major Rossiter felt himself trembling. It began in the calves of his legs and spread up his body to his chest, making breathing difficult.

Five children! A paddling pool! Racing cars! It was monstrous! His peace and privacy would be shattered. Not only that, the value of his property, on which he had spent a great deal of time and money, would be considerably diminished.

But it was the loss of the view which distressed him most. It was his view. No-one had any right to build a four bedroomed house between him and it without asking his permission first which, of course, he would never for a moment consider giving.

Almost without thinking, he found himself thrusting his hand into his inside pocket where he kept his cheque book.

"I'll buy the field," he said abruptly. "How much did you want? Two thousand, wasn't it?"

Blower's eyes lit up but he made a deprecatory gesture with one hand.

"Sorry, Major, but I can't accept it. If it was up to me, I'd say 'yes' like a shot. After all, your money's as good as the next man's. But I've already given first refusal to this other bloke, see, and taken his deposit. I don't like going back on my word."

His word! Major Rossiter thought. Good God above, the snivelling little scoundrel actually has the gall to talk about his word.

"Very well," he replied, letting his hand drop down by his side. "But I'd like to make it clear, Blower, that I have no intention of letting the matter rest there."

Although as he said the words, he had no idea precisely what action he might take, the remark was nevertheless intended as a veiled threat. Blower, however, whether out of obtuseness or tact, did not appear to recognise it as such.

Smiling and almost bustling in his eagerness, he hurried forward to open the door.

"I'll be in touch, Major Rossiter," he promised. "In the meantime, I'll have a word with this other bloke and see if something can't be worked out. After all, I feel if anyone ought to have that field, it should be you, seeing as it's right next door to your place."

"Thank you, Mr Blower," Major Rossiter said stiffly and, getting into the car, drove off.

His first action on returning home was to inspect the field at close quarters by climbing over the fence, pushing aside the horse as he did so. He was well aware that he was trespassing but he was past caring about such legal niceties. He had to know exactly what he was up against. As in any battle, it is of primary importance to spy out the enemy's position before engaging in combat.

It was as he had feared. The little wooden pegs marked out a large area in the centre of the paddock. Standing in the middle of it, he looked first to his left where the slope of lawn and shrubbery rose gently towards the rear façade of Charmont

Villa and the big rectangle of glass, glittering in the sun, which formed the picture window of his drawing room.

Turning to his right, he surveyed the view, as bright and as clear in the gentle spring sunshine as if it had been newly created that morning.

Tender, he thought. That was the word he was looking for. *Tender*.

The stern winter outlines of the woods and hedgerows were faintly brushed over with green where the new leaves were breaking while the river lay quiet, coiled up as if asleep in its valley, silver backed and motionless.

Looking at it, Major Rossiter felt himself trembling again; not with anger this time but with a new passion which he could not define. It was more than love. Certainly he had never experienced such a feeling for a woman. It was deeper than that; holier, if you like; similar to the *frisson* which ran through his blood whenever he heard his regimental band play their slow march.

It was as if his whole soul went out to encompass that sweeping vista, cleansing his vision so that he saw it all, even the smallest detail, with a new clarity and filling him with a powerful sense of purpose.

Oh, no! he thought, whacking his stick down on to the ground as he walked away. He had no intention of giving in without a fight. The enemy was at the gates; no foreign foe this time but traitors from within; men like Blower, seedy little barbarians in dirty overalls who were prepared to sell their birthright, as well as other people's, for a couple of thousand pounds.

His solicitor, whom he consulted that afternoon, was not very helpful.

"Pity you didn't buy the field when it was first offered to you," he remarked. "As for the present situation, there's not a lot you can do. Once the paddock's sold, you can always object to planning permission being given."

"But would I win?" Major Rossiter demanded.

The solicitor looked doubtful.

"That's a moot point. It would depend on how many other people raise objections."

Major Rossiter heard him out although what he had to

say was of little comfort to him. He could not even claim compensation for the damage the horse had done to his shrubs, the fence at the bottom of the garden being his responsibility—as the deeds, held by his solicitor, showed on examination.

As for organizing a protest, the Major realized it would be futile. As only his enjoyment of the view would be ruined, it was highly improbable that anyone else in the village would support him.

Not even the vicar, Major Rossiter thought gloomily.

So it was to be single combat between himself and Blower and, for the moment at least, Blower, as owner of the field, had the advantage.

But he did not seem eager to use it for, over the next few days, nothing happened although the Major kept the field under constant surveillance from the observation post he had set up in the back bedroom where, from its window, he had a clear view of the paddock through his binoculars.

It was on the following Sunday that there were the first signs of enemy action. Blower arrived, driving his battered little green van into the field. Having parked it, he caught the horse and led it into the shed where its long, mournful, white face could be seen sticking out over the bottom half of the stable door. Blower then walked into the centre of the paddock to inspect the pegs, strolling round their perimeter with his hands in his pockets and a jaunty look to the set of his shoulders.

Shortly afterwards, a second vehicle arrived, a large, flashy estate car. The greasy-haired man in the bright navy-blue suit got out and joined Blower in the centre of the field where the two men shook hands.

A trembling in his own hands made it difficult for Major Rossiter to focus the binoculars. They jiggled and shook while, behind the lenses, his eyes misted over.

Very carefully, he wiped his eyes before lifting the binoculars again, holding them steady by propping his elbows on the window-sill.

He now had the two men in sharp focus. Blower was smiling, that cocky, know-all, infuriating grin. The other man was smiling too as if well pleased.

It was quite clear to the Major that what he was witnessing

was the final declaration of victory between the pair of them. The battle was over; the field was theirs.

But not quite! Major Rossiter thought grimly. In order for a victory to be complete, there had to be total surrender and, as far as he was concerned, he had not yet shown the white flag.

Letting the binoculars drop down on their strap against his chest, he rose to his feet.

It was Mrs Rossiter's alarmed exclamations which drew the attention of the two men to the figure of the Major striding down the lawn towards them, clutching a shot gun and trying to fend off his wife with his other arm as she ran distractedly beside him, crying out, "Please, George, I beg you, don't do anything foolish!"

"Out of my way, woman!" the Major was shouting.

He came to a halt in front of the rhododendrons where he laid the gun across his forearm as Blower, still wearing that ingratiating smile, now a little fixed and nervous, came forward to meet him.

"Now, come on, Major Rossiter," he began in a voice of sweet reasonableness, "we don't want any bother, do we? Put the gun down and we'll talk business. If you want the field that badly, I'll sell it to you."

"How much?" the Major demanded.

Blower hesitated, glancing back over his shoulder to the other man as if confirming some secret pact between them.

When he turned back, his eyes were very bright as he fixed them on the Major.

"Shall we say two thousand five hundred, seeing as how there's another buyer in the market?"

What happened next was open to dispute.

At his trial, Major Rossiter stated that he raised the gun merely as a threatening gesture with no intention of pulling the trigger. It was his wife who, by grabbing it, caused it to go off, a statement with which Phoebe, almost incoherent, agreed.

Whatever the truth of the matter, the barrel swung upwards, the trigger was pulled and Blower, still wearing the smile, staggered backwards, a large red hole suddenly springing up in the middle of his overall bib.

The sound of the shot echoed across the field, frightening

the horse which kicked and trampled inside the stable, adding its terrified neighs to the deafening reverberations.

Oddly enough, the Major observed, frowning as he concentrated his attention on the sprawled figure of Blower as it lay on the grass—such an insignificant little man even in death—the view remained unaltered. He had thought for a moment that the whole vista might come tumbling down, meadow and pasture, wood and river, shattered into pieces by the shock of the explosion, like a huge picture painted on glass.

But it remained untouched, serene in the spring sunshine. *Tender*, that was the word.

Somewhere on the periphery of his consciousness, he was aware of a woman screaming and a man's voice shouting, "You crazy fool! Look what you've done! You've shot my brother!"

"What's that you say?" Major Rossiter asked, drawing himself up to attention on the far side of the rhododendrons.

The man looked up as he knelt by the body.

"I told you. He's my brother. I wasn't going to buy the bloody field from him. We set it up between us to force up the price."

"No house then?" the Major demanded.

The man shook his head and turned back to his dead brother, trying vainly to loosen the neck of his collar.

"Rather a waste of time," the Major commented, half to himself.

He meant not just the man's actions but the whole affair, his part in it as well as Blower's.

Dead ground, he thought. All that trouble to capture a piece of territory which was not in enemy hands in the first place.

But that was the irony as well as the futility of war.

AND TURN THE HOUR

Peter Godfrey

THE WORLD SMILED. It was warm, and it smiled, and its warmth prickled through his eyelids, behind his eyes, and there was another warmth inside that prickled up to meet it. An excitement, a lazy grasshopper springing of memories. New memories. The money, first. No more grind, no more debt, no more working for other people. And then Heath. Yes, Heath in his arms, her eyes bright but her lower lip tremulous in the ecstasy of saying yes. Last night. Wonderful night. And now the sun was shining. This year 1984 had become a wonderful time.

He bought a new watch. On impulse. There was some sort of symbolism there, but nothing deep. New life—new watch. He came out of the shop like a schoolboy with a holiday, unstrapping his old watch, dropping it carefully into his left-hand trouser pocket. He put the new one on his wrist, and adjusted the hands to conform with the clock in the tower of the Cape Town City Hall. 10.55. He started to wind.

A vague cloud passed through his mind. He should have wound first, of course. Maybe a minute. . . . He looked at the City Hall clock again, and then down at his wrist. 11.47. And they both gave the same time.

He felt a nausea of imbalance, and then his mind reeled in a drunken clutch of hope. This was his old watch on his wrist. He must have put the new one in his pocket. A mistake of some kind. Some kind of mistake.

His hand reached into his pocket, fingers groping, pulling out the contents. He looked. An unused cinema ticket and a crushed white flower trembled in his palm. He had never seen them before.

The warmth behind his eyelids turned into a shaft of cold, a bitter piercing shaft, and the other cold inside him welled up to meet it, icily strangling the memories of the money, of Heath. The world shivered and twisted.

And snarled.

"And that is all he can remember," said Dr Beresky. He shook his lined head gently, and his large ears trembled in an incipient flap. He added: "I am very worried about him"

Rolf le Roux leaned forward sympathetically, and held his pipe for a moment away from his beard. "I still don't understand," he said, "why you have come to me."

Beresky answered his question only obliquely. He said: "Let me tell you something about amnesia. First, it is brought on by a trauma—a shock. Second, when an amnesia victim visits a psychiatrist, he already wants to be cured, and so he is well on the way to curing himself. All I have to do is show him the right road." He cleared his throat. "Young Winters came to me of his own accord, it is true, but there are still undeniable signs that he does not wish to be cured. Yes, I say that even though he is tortured by the idea that without a cure he will go mad, that he will lose the girl to whom he has just become engaged, and all the benefits of the large sum of money he has just inherited."

Rolf asked: "Have you any idea why he does not want to be cured?"

"Yes, but only in very general terms. I can say, with some certainty that he does not want to remember what happened in the missing 47 minutes, because the event or events which caused the shock are too unpleasant for him to face." He hesitated. "That much one can say of amnesia generally, but in Winters' case the resistance to remembering is so strong, the cause must have been something . . . unthinkable."

Rolf prompted again: "And you have come to me?"

"Because you stay in the same lodging house as Winters, and he is fond of you and has confidence in you. Perhaps you can help break down his resistance. And then again, you have a connection with the police."

"In what way is that useful?"

"Mr le Roux, if it would only be possible for us to find out where Winters went during the missing period, exactly what he did—"

Rolf said: "That may be more difficult than you think. After all, the trail is five days old. But I am quite prepared to try."

"Thank you," said Beresky, and hesitated again. "Perhaps the police would know of some incident, some violent incident, which happened at that time, which he might have seen or been involved in. If so—"

"It is worth looking into, Dr Beresky, but anything violent would certainly have got into the newspapers, and I have seen nothing there. No. But there are other things which may help. Let us see. We know certain details about the period. We know that at the outset something happened to destroy Winters' balance of mind. We know that he was in Plein Street or the immediate vicinity at the time. We know that after that he did certain things—he rid himself of the new watch and put the old one on his wrist, he acquired a cinema ticket and a flower, a white lily. These things, I should imagine, must bear some relationship, some sort of pattern, tying in with the shock that caused the mental imbalance?"

"Definitely."

"And in your treatment you yourself have discovered nothing more about any of these individual items?"

"Nothing that sheds any real light on the matter to me. But perhaps if you. . . . Look, Mr le Roux, I will be attending to Winters at 2.30 this afternoon. If you would like to be present, it might have a helpful influence. As things stand, I do not see what harm it could do. Personally, I am at a dead end."

The call from Detective Sergeant Johnson came while Rolf was still in the waiting-room of the nursing home.

"Nothing," said Johnson. "No complaints at all from the vicinity of Plein Street—in fact, there was no crime of violence at all in central Cape Town during daylight hours that day. There was a fight between some drunken sailors at the bottom of Adderley Street just about 6 p.m., but I don't suppose that qualifies."

Rolf said: "No. The incident, whatever it was, must have occurred near Plein Street between say 10.45 and noon. And it must have been sufficiently horrible to make a normal young-ster lose his memory. That's all I can tell you at the moment. Perhaps this afternoon . . . I will get in touch with you again later. And what about street accidents? Have you checked them?"

"Yes. No luck there either. Still, there may have been one unreported. I'll try the hospitals for you this afternoon. Will you give me a ring at Caledon Square just before six?"

As Rolf hung up, Dr Beresky came bustling up.

Donald Winters lay fully dressed on a couch in the room. He looked up as they entered, but slowly, as though his muscles were rustily responding to habit, and his thoughts were somewhere in the distance.

"Your old friend Mr le Roux is here," said Beresky. "He is trying to help us."

Winters said: "Hello, Rolf." Again it was a slow reflex action; his voice was expressionless, unmeaning. All the same, in brief tantalizing flashes, panic chased hope across his eyes. Rolf thought of those eyes as he had last seen them—alert and full of fun. He took one of the chairs at the side of the couch.

Beresky took the other. He rolled up the boy's right sleeve, found a vein, and inserted the needle of a hypodermic syringe. He explained: "I am injecting sodium pentothal, an hypnotic drug. It helps release the inhibitions. Donald, will you please start counting?"

Winters said: "One, two, three, four . . . five . . . shix." His voice blurred sleepily. Beresky ceased his slow pressure on the plunger. He started to talk, slowly and distinctly.

"Donald, think back to when you were walking down Plein Street. You were very happy because you had inherited money and just become engaged. You passed a jeweller's shop, turned in, and bought a watch. Then what did you do?"

"I put . . . the new . . . on wrist . . . the old in . . . pocket."

"And then?"

"Adjust time. With clock. Wind watch."

"Go on."

"Looked at clock again. Time . . . had changed."

Beresky said: "Listen carefully. Time doesn't just change. Hours don't vanish into thin air. Between the times the clock changed you did things, saw things. You know that, don't you?"

The boy on the couch moved his head from side to side. He groaned.

Beresky persisted: "You know that, don't you? Answer me."

The boy said: "God, leave . . . alone." His left hand started to clench and unclench.

"What did you do? What did you see?"

Winters tried weakly to pull his right wrist out of Beresky's grasp. He flexed his knees, rolled his head. He opened his mouth as though he was going to shout, but the voice that emerged was barely a whisper: "No."

Only the one syllable, but it had as undertones indescribable tortures.

Beresky mopped his own forehead. "All right, boy," he said. "I won't ask you again. Not now, anyway. Relax. That's right. Nobody's going to hurt you. Good. Now we're going to have another little experiment. You won't even have to think this time. When I ask you a question, just tell me what comes into your mind. Ready?"

"Yes."

"Then here's the first word: 'Watch'?"

The boy hardly hesitated: "Life."

"Don't just answer with a single word," said Beresky. "Tell me *everything* that comes into your mind. Now, let's try again: Flower?"

The boy remained silent.

Beresky repeated: "Flower?"

"Verse."

"Go on."

"Flower. Verse. White. Pure." The last two words came then, bursting from his lips: "No blood!"

"All right, Donald. Easy, now. Think of a special kind of flower. A lily. That's your word—lily."

Winters said: "Lily . . . of Laguna. Lagoon. Sea. Muizenberg. Sand. White sand. White hand." He began to move his head again.

Beresky pressed him: "White hand?"

The boy moaned.

"White?"

"Clean. Pure."

"And hand?"

The boy screamed.

Beresky came with Rolf out into the sunlight. The psychiatrist said: "You see now what I mean when I say the shock he experienced must have been horrible? And violent?"

"Horror is relative," said Rolf. "The simplest acts may have an element of horror to the individual. I, for example, hate to kill spiders . . . it is a question of a particular type of upbringing and personal experiences. But you are right—what shocked the hour loose from Winters' life is associated with violence. With the shedding of blood. And yet there were no crimes of violence that day."

"Are you certain of that?"

"Almost certain. I will know for sure tonight. . . . Look, Doctor, doesn't the fiancée stay near here? Maybe she can help."

He walked slowly down the road.

The apartment building was ultra-modern, all chrome and glass, and the girl who answered his ring was refreshing in her naturalness. She wore her hair long and loose, and dressed with that artless simplicity which is the truest smartness. She had been crying.

Rolf introduced himself, explained the purpose of his visit. She said: "Oh yes, Mr le Roux. Donald has often spoken of you. Come inside, please. This is my brother Arthur."

The sullen, powerfully built man stood up, and extended a perfunctory hand in greeting. "Sorry I can't stay," he said, and then: "If you're going to talk about Winters, I can't be any use." His voice was both unpleasant and impatient. He went out.

Heath Cooper said: "Tell me, Mr le Roux, is Donald any better?"

Rolf took a deep pull at his pipe. "Let me explain. Donald has lost his memory because of some deep shock he experienced that morning. If I can find out what caused that shock . . ."

She shook her head helplessly. "I didn't see him at all. I had an appointment with my dressmaker. We had arranged to meet in the afternoon, but of course—"

"And you can think of nothing that might have put him in a state of mind where a shock might be accentuated? Did you get the impression that he was worried? Think hard, Heath."

"Nothing. All his worries had gone. He'd just inherited his money. We'd just become engaged. We were both very happy. More happy, I suppose, than most couples, because . . . well, if it hadn't been for the money, Donald would never have asked me to marry him."

"Why not?"

"Well, probably on account of my brother—really my half-brother. He and Donald don't like each other, as you might have noticed. Arthur's a rich man, and he supports me. Donald didn't realize I'd cheerfully have given everything up just to be with him. He had some silly pride that made him keep silent until he could afford to give me everything that Arthur . . . but of course the inheritance cleared up that barrier."

"I see. And how long have you known Donald?"

"Just over a year."

"And did he talk freely to you about his past life?"

"Yes. He's a very frank sort of person. I think he's told me . . . most things."

Rolf said: "I am going to mention a few words. See if any of them strikes a chord in connection with anything Donald has ever told you. Concentrate. I'll say them slowly."

"I'm ready."

"Right. Here they are, then: Flower. Muizenberg. Hand. Blood."

She leaned forward in bewilderment. "Nothing. Nothing at all."

Rolf looked at his watch as he came out of the apartment building, and walked briskly to a taxi-rank. He gave the driver the address of his and the boy's lodgings. Once there, he spoke persuasively to the proprietor, got from him a key, and let himself into the boy's room.

For a moment he stood irresolute. In his mind he heard Beresky say "Flower" and the blurred voice answer "Verse". He moved to the bookcase.

There were two volumes of poetry, one by William Morris and the other by Kipling. He took both books to the table. He thought of going through them for an hour or so; then he remembered an old trick He allowed both books to fall open naturally. The William Morris book fell open at "The Haystack in the Floods". Before reading, he turned his eyes to the Kipling volume, and suddenly prickled in discovery. The page that faced him carried a poem called "The Flowers".

He read it through carefully, word by word. Then, with the stem of his pipe, he scored the page next to the third verse:

"Buy my English posies:
Here's to match your need—
Buy a tuft of royal heath
Buy a bunch of weed
White as sand of Muizenberg
Spun before the gale—
Buy my heath and lilies
And I'll tell you whence you hail.
Under hot Constantia broad the vineyards lie;
Throned and thorned the aching berg props the speckless sky;
Slow below the Wynberg firs trails the tilted wain:
Take the flower, and turn the hour, and kiss your love again."

In his mind Rolf began to see the dim outlines of a pattern, and he did not like what he saw. He went over the words again. "Royal heath", he said to himself, and then "Heath and lilies". The word "white" leaped at him from the context. He remembered the boy's association—"pure"—and he saw again Heath Cooper and the appeal in her eyes. And then he remembered the boy's next words, the horror-stricken cry: "No blood!" Some of the horror seeped into him.

The pattern began to take shape.

He took the volume with him, locked the door, and went down the passage to his own room. He sat by the telephone for some time before he dialled. He asked for Johnson.

The voice came through.

"That you, Rolf? No luck at all. No hospital cases unreported—nothing. I think—"

"No, that's all right, Johnson. There's something else, now.

This boy's name is Donald Winters—make a note of that. I want you to find out if there's any record of him being involved in a murder case some time in the past. Wait, I can give you some more details. The murder was one where the victim bled a lot, and it must have happened over a year ago. Yes, I would say well over a year. . . ."

On his way to Caledon Square, Rolf stopped off at the Post Office. He looked at the long rank of the flower stalls, alive with colour and morning sunlight, and rubbed his beard contemplatively.

A coloured woman brandished a fragrant bunch under his nose. "Only 20 cents, Master," she said, "only 20 cents."

She looked bright-eyed and intelligent.

"I have a Rand for you," said Rolf, "if you can find me the flower-seller who sold one white lily to a young man last Friday morning, and there will be another Rand for this person."

"Yes, Master." She bustled off, talking to this stall and that. In a short while she was back with a man, who looked at Rolf suspiciously. He said: "I sold a young man a white lily last Friday morning. What does the Master want to know?"

"Everything you can tell me about it."

"He asked for a lily, and I sold it to him. That is all." The man was uncomfortable; he was holding his left hand very firmly in his pocket.

On inspiration Rolf said: "I am not from the police, and you may keep the watch." He took out an additional note, and the coloured man thawed visibly.

He said. "I think the young Master was mad. He did not want a bunch of flowers. He said he must have just one lily, and it must be pure white. I found one and he gave me 10 cents for it. Then I saw him standing on the corner, and he squashed the lily in his hand and put it in his pocket. I did not see him after that."

Rolf handed over the notes. He prompted: "And what about the watch?"

"He had two watches, Master, an old one and a new one. He was holding them both in his left hand while he was talking to me. After he crushed the flower, he put the old watch back on his wrist and dropped the new one in the gutter. I picked it up. If the young Master had come back, I——"

"It is all right," said Rolf. "He does not want it any more."

Round the corner, in Plein Street, he took the ticket from his wallet, and showed it at the box-office of the Nostalgia Cinema where it had been purchased. The hard blonde gave a cursory glance at it, and spoke before he could say anything: "No returns. You should have gone in when you bought the ticket."

"This is not my ticket," said Rolf. "I am from the police, and I am making certain enquiries. Do you remember selling this ticket to a young man last Friday morning?"

"Mister," said the blonde, "I sell 500 tickets to young men every morning, and if you line them all up in front of me five minutes later, I still wouldn't be able to swear to any one of them."

Rolf persisted: "But this young man did not go into the cinema. Don't you remember anything about that?"

"I wouldn't, but Jimmy might. Jimmy!"

The uniformed man at the door came over. Rolf explained again.

"Come to think of it," said Jimmy, "I do remember something. Young guy with fair hair?"

"Yes."

"Well, he acted a bit screwy. He bought the ticket, all right, and then came over to look at the poster. We had a featurette on that day which was also advertised—a 'Crime Does Not Pay' short—and he seemed to be peering at the announcement. All of a sudden he just turned and walked quickly down the street."

"You only show vintage films. Do you remember what was the feature that day?"

"Last Friday? Wait a minute. Abbott and Costello . . . no, that was on Thursday only. Roy Rogers was on at the beginning of the week. I've got it—Burt Lancaster."

"And the title of the picture?"

" 'Kiss the Blood off my Hands'."

The pattern was balanced, complete. Except for the murder. And Johnson had unearthed the particulars.

It had happened 27 months before. The victim was a young man named Clyde Parsons, and his throat had been cut in the dining room of his apartment in Fresnaye. There were signs of a slight struggle; Parsons had been forced back on to a table before the murderer could effect the lethal cut. The weapon was left on the floor, but it had been wiped clean of finger-prints. Blood had spurted all over the room.

And Donald Winters?

"Clyde Parsons was a great friend of mine," he had said in his statement, "and I was in the habit of letting myself into his apartment without knocking. I did not have a key, and the door was always locked when Parsons was out.

"On the evening of August 17, at approximately 8 p.m., I called round at Parsons' rooms. I could hear the radio playing inside and the door was unlocked, so I was surprised not to find any lights burning. I had just turned on the switch when I was struck over the head and lost consciousness. I recovered consciousness only two hours later under the care of the police surgeon.

"I did not see the person who struck me. All I saw before I was struck was a hand covered with blood holding an iron poker. Apart from the blood, I am unable to remember whether there was anything distinctive about the hand, but I do have the feeling that there was some abnormality about it which I have forgotten, and which I will recognize if I ever see the hand again.

"Parsons was very popular and to the best of my knowledge had no enemies. However, when I had seen him the day before, he had mentioned he had worries in connection with someone called Prentice."

With his thumbnail Johnson underlined the last sentence. "And this name," he said, "is the most interesting feature of the whole case."

"Why so?"

"We've heard of it in other connections. Nothing definite, you understand. Scraps of reported conversation, and a couple of anonymous letters, but enough to convince us that this Prentice, whoever he or she may be, is a very remarkable black-mailer. We even know some of the victims, but at this stage nobody is prepared to come forward with a definite charge."

"Why do you say Prentice may be a woman?"

"Well, there's nothing in any of our information to definitely indicate sex, so I'm just covering every contingency. Besides, I've always found women turn more readily to blackmail than men."

Rolf grinned. "It seems to me you know the wrong type of women," he said, and then: "But seriously, I think I can find Prentice for you. Only there will be no evidence."

"Yes? And will there be any possible grounds which might justify a temporary arrest?"

"I think so."

"Then you needn't worry about evidence. If I can show Prentice under lock and key to a certain woman, and promise her complete anonymity, then she'll talk. And we'll also hear from some of the others. When can we make this arrest?"

Rolf said: "Tomorrow morning, I think. . . . I will telephone you tonight with details. But you will have to promise to do exactly what I say. There are more things at stake than the arrest of a murderer."

But before he caught the bus he telephoned Heath. And he chose the telephone booth on the corner of Plein Street, near the jeweller's shop where Donald Winters had bought his watch.

He asked her questions, and knew the answers before she gave them.

"Yes. My dressmaker has a room in a building on the corner of Plein Street. Murray House. She's on the second floor. And yes, we did stand talking on her balcony for quite a while."

In his room, Rolf thought again of the problem and its two aspects . . . the past and the future. The past he knew, every twist and nook and cranny, but when he thought of the future his mind was shadowy, groping. It was possible that success on the one side would lead to disaster on the other. He did not know enough to decide such a momentous matter for himself. It was a decision for a specialist.

Regretfully, he decided it would be better if he shared his information. He hoped Dr Beresky would approve of his plan.

He reached stubby fingers for the telephone directory.

The bell was pressed long and loud. The time was seven in the morning.

Inside there was a muttered curse, and then the door was opened violently by a man in pyjamas and dressing-gown. There were traces of shaving lather on his face. He said: "What in hell do you want?"

The fresh-complexioned man standing in the forefront of the group asked: "Mr Arthur Cooper?"

"Yes?"

"I am Detective Sergeant Johnson of the Cape Town C.I.D. I believe you know Mr le Roux, Dr Beresky and Mr Winters. I am sorry we've knocked you up so early in the morning, but we were anxious to find both you and your sister at home. There is an urgent matter to discuss."

Cooper hesitated. "Well, come on. What is this urgent business?"

Johnson looked at Rolf, who said: "I will explain." He settled himself in a chair, and his eyes moved from Cooper to Winters to Heath.

He said: "You all know that Donald is suffering from amnesia. There is an hour missing out of his life. The investigation of what happened in that hour has led straight back to a murder which was committed over two years ago. Donald was a witness. He walked into the victim's rooms before the murderer had left, and was knocked unconscious. All he saw was a bloodstained hand holding a poker just before he was hit. But there was something about that hand that made him know he would recognize it if he saw it again. Some sort of physical difference to other hands. And a physical difference that was not apparent normally, but only when the hand was *gripping* something."

"What has that got to do with us?" said Cooper impatiently.

"I will tell you," said Rolf. "The morning when Donald fell ill, he looked at a balcony and saw a hand gripping the railing. It was a hand with the same infirmity as the one which had gripped the poker on the night of the murder. When he saw to whom the hand belonged, the balance of his mind was upset."

Heath asked: "Whose hand was it?"

Rolf looked at her steadily. He said: "Yours."

Heath started: "Oh no, I . . . ," and then Arthur Cooper interrupted fiercely: "What nonsense is this? Winters, is this the story you have told them?"

The boy's eyes twitched in panic.

Rolf said: "He has told us nothing. He still does not remember. But it is the only explanation of the facts. He lost his memory because he associated his fiancée with the murderer of his best friend."

Cooper turned again to Rolf. "What sort of a case do you think you are building up? Heath wouldn't harm a fly. Even if Winters did confirm your imaginative reasoning—and that is all it can be—even if he did confirm it, I say, it would prove nothing. He made a mistake, that's all."

"He did make a mistake," said Rolf. "His fiancée didn't murder Clyde Parsons. She couldn't have. The crime was never committed by a woman. A man did it, a man powerful enough to overpower a strong victim, force him backward on to a table, and then cut his throat."

Cooper looked shocked. "Then why this picking on Heath . . . ?"

"Just because Donald did make a mistake. Because of the abnormality in the hand. An abnormality which would be an impossible coincidence if shared between her and some stranger . . . *but one which might be perfectly natural in a blood relative*."

Cooper blustered: "Have you now got the impudence to accuse me?"

"Yes. But you can easily prove your innocence if you want to. Are you prepared to grip this length of wood I have here, and let Heath grip it too, so we can compare results?"

"No," said Cooper, and laughed again. "Why should I submit myself to a test which is based entirely on a theory . . . unconfirmed even by the man you say provided the basis of the theory? No, I will not do it, and you cannot compel me to."

"That is quite true," said Rolf meekly, and added: "But there is one other theory on which I am prepared to stand or fall. You see, Mr Cooper, the name of the murderer is known. It is the same name as a mysterious person who makes a living from blackmail. It is obviously not his real name, and yet there must have been a reason for choosing it."

Cooper said sarcastically, "What alias am I supposed to have adopted? And what tortuous reason have you concocted for that choice?"

Rolf ignored him. He said, quietly, "Heath, my dear, I am sorry about this—but it may be our only chance to help Donald. Do you mind answering one or two questions?"

"No."

"I am pleased. Now, listen: you told me last time I was here that Arthur Cooper is your half-brother?"

"Yes."

"You share the same name, and so it would be natural to assume that you shared the same father. But my theory is that the connecting link between you is your mother. I say that your mother was married twice, that Arthur was the son of the first husband, and that he used his step-father's name when your mother remarried. Am I right or wrong, Heath?"

"Right."

"Then, Heath, do you know the name of your mother's first husband, of Arthur's father?"

"Yes."

"And what was that name?"

"Prentice."

The door closed on Johnson and his prisoner.

The boy still sat in lethargic fearfulness. Incongruously, a sobbing Heath ran to him for consolation. She put her arm round his shoulders and, barely perceptibly, he flinched. His eyes welcomed and sought escape.

Beresky and Rolf came to stand in front of him.

Beresky said: "Donald?"

"Yes?"

"You heard the talk in this room? You saw what happened?"

"Yes. But I don't . . . understand. This suspicion of Heath. I don't remember. . . ."

"But you will, Donald, you will. There's just one thing for you to do. Fill your mind with it, Donald. Concentrate. Just on this one point: Heath is innocent. Say it."

"Heath is innocent."

"*Proved* innocent, Donald. You made a mistake. Just a mistake. And Heath is innocent. Your mind is full of that? Now try to remember."

The boy's muscles tensed. His head lolled. His lips twisted to form the word "innocent".

Beresky nodded to Rolf who, suddenly and resonantly, began to quote:

"Under hot Constantia broad the vineyards lie;
Throned and thorned the aching berg props the speckless sky;
Slow below the Wynberg firs trails the tilted wain—
Take the flower, and turn the hour, and kiss your love again."

Beresky said: "Think!"

The boy bared his teeth, moaned, and moved his eyes in bafflement.

Rolf said, very slowly: "Take the flower. And turn the hour. And kiss your love again."

Winters' face shivered into a spasm. His muscles moved, twisted and sagged. Tears shot from his eyes.

"I remember now," he said.

He came from the shop, dropping the old watch into his left-hand trouser pocket, fitting the new on his wrist. He adjusted it to the clock on the City Hall, and started to wind. The time was 10.55.

A vague cloud passed through his mind. He should have wound it first, of course. Maybe a minute . . . He looked up again at the City Hall, but something stopped the sweep of his eyes.

A hand. Clutching a balcony rail. But not just any hand. A hand with a strange little finger which stuck out almost at right angles as it gripped. The same hand that had reached out to bludgeon him. The hand that had been red with Clyde Parsons' blood. No doubt of that. And now he had the murderer. And now—

The hand moved, turned, bringing the body to which it

belonged out of the shadows, showing the face clearly in the shattering light.

He felt his feet shuffling, walking away with him, and he was surprised he was not staggering. As he was surprised he was not screaming aloud from the torment in his mind.

He walked to the top of Plein Street. And down again.

He thought of her always as a flower, as a white flower, like the heath in the poem. White and pure. "White as sands of Muizenberg." With white hands, pure hands. But they had once been red. . . .

With Clyde's blood.

He had not sworn an oath—nothing so melodramatic as that. All the same there had been the *feeling* . . . if he ever found the murderer. . . .

And now . . . God!

He loved Heath so much. So much.

He had noticed the poster as he passed the first time, and now it seemed to bore into his brain with a new meaning. "Kiss the Blood off my Hands." Kiss the blood off Heath's hands. . . . Maybe there was some way. . . .

He crossed the road with long strides, and bought a ticket from the hard-faced blonde in the box. But somehow the poster drew him. He went to it, peered at the strip pasted across the bottom, and stiffened with shock.

"Crime Does Not Pay."

No escape. There it was again. The problem. His own problem that he would have to face.

He wandered. And did not know he was wandering.

He stripped the watch off his wrist, and fetched the old one out of his pocket. Old and new. Old without Heath. New with. . . . And then he saw the lilies.

The poem came back to him. "Buy my heath and lilies." Both white. Heath . . . and lilies. And here were lilies.

He looked at them, and again the poem came, like a command: "Take the flower." He took one.

It lay in his right palm, a symbol of purity. And then suddenly the curves of the bloom reminded him of a hand, a white hand, with a little finger that stuck out strangely when it gripped.

He crushed it.

And became conscious of the watches he was holding. Old life, new life. He dropped the new life in the gutter.

But the poem persisted, even though he walked. "Take the flower, and turn the hour, and kiss your love again."

Kiss your love with the bloodstained hands.

Back, back, back. Back again to where it happened, here on the corner of Plein Street. Only she has gone. There is no hand now on the balcony rail.

"And turn the hour."

If only one could. Back again to 10.55. And the rest be a dream, yes, that would be a solution. Back to 10.55. And no hand on the balcony rail. No hand to meet his eye as it climbed to the City Hall tower, no hand because the hand was a dream, and the clock shows 10.55. The clock *will* show 10.55. . . .

The clock showed 11.47. And his watch. But—?

The old watch, of course. A mistake. . . .

He put his hand into his pocket, and pulled out an unused cinema ticket and a crushed white flower.

He had never seen them before.

TRUTH TO TELL

Penelope Wallace

MERIAM WAS A compulsive liar. She lied about the small things in life: "Yes, my hair's naturally blonde"—with brown roots. "I'm just 22"—she was 24. "My boyfriend, John Manners, has a high position in the bank"—he was a cashier. "Of course we don't sleep together; we're getting married". The former statement was false but the latter was true. For John Manners was in love with Meriam—lies and all and, when she said she loved him, he knew it was so. She also told him that he was the greatest lover since Casanova and, here, male vanity assured him, she spoke the truth. As to the large things of life, she had loved her parents—and told them so—and she loved John Manners. In twenty-four years no other large things had come her way.

Meriam had a flatlet in "Maida Vale"—postal district Kilburn—and here she produced dinner for John—"I'm proud of my cooking"—on Tuesdays, Wednesdays and Thursdays. On Mondays they went to the cinema, on Fridays they queued for the theatre, Saturdays and Sundays they drove into the country in John's old Ford. Sometimes Tuesday's routine was disturbed by John's visit to his parents. He would press Meriam to go with him but, like many liars, she knew she was not believed and fear kept her away.

It was on a Wednesday following such a Tuesday that Meriam's life changed.

"I tried to ring you when I got back to the flat, but there was no answer."

"I was in all evening."

"Well, I rang twice."

"You must have dialled the wrong number."

"No, Meriam, I don't mind you going out, but why say you were in when . . ."

He was interrupted by a knock at the door. Meriam opened it. An elderly lady stepped in, peered at John, and started to speak.

"Forgive me for coming in when you've got a visitor, but you left your knitting pattern behind yesterday evening and I thought . . ." She smiled vaguely and trotted off. When the door closed, John turned to Meriam: "I think it was very sweet of you to go and sit with the couple next door, but why couldn't you have told me when I said I rang you? Why did you lie?"

"I don't know," she admitted and went into the kitchenette to check on the progress of the dinner.

"And another thing," said John when she reappeared, "why aren't you wearing your glasses?"

"I don't need them any more—the optician said . . ."

He took her arms and pulled her gently to him.

"Darling," he said, "you look beautiful in glasses—please wear them."

"I'll put them on later—I must bring in the dinner. I've made something really special and it'll be overcooked." And she broke away from him and went back to the kitchenette. He heard the clatter of dishes, and then she was coming through the archway with the tray. As he went forward to help her, he thought how beautiful she looked in her blue Kaftan.

It happened suddenly. She crossed towards the table, caught her foot on the stool, and crash. . . .

She lay still and silent, and he knelt beside her to wipe the Vesta beef curry off her white face, and the Marks and Spencer cheesecake from the lids of her faulty blue eyes. He waited for those blue eyes to open, for her to say that someone had moved the footstool. . . . She lay very still, and when he felt her wrist the pulse seemed faint. She must have hit her head as she fell. . . .

The ambulance came at last and John, clasping Meriam's handbag, rode with the stretcher to the hospital. There were endless X-rays and, finally, he was told that Meriam was in no danger and would probably regain consciousness in the early hours of the morning. He was told to go home; but he waited on the hard bench until finally a nurse told him he could see her for a moment. Some colour had come back to her face and she opened her blue eyes and smiled at him. It was a smile he was to remember. He went home, showered, changed, and set out for the bank.

Even banks have hearts and, after having recounted fifty pounds three times, the story of the accident came out and he was sent home. On the way he phoned the hospital and was told that Meriam was sleeping and he could come and see her at six p.m. He set the alarm for five and fell into bed.

She was sitting up when he arrived—wearing her glasses and chatting to the nurse. "Well, actually my name's Mary, but I've always preferred Meriam—Oh, hello John. I was just telling nurse what a fool I'd been trying to carry that tray without my glasses—and what a waste of good food—of course I'm a rotten cook but you can get excellent packet food. Maybe I should go to cookery classes on Tuesday evenings."

"You see," said the nurse, "she's her old self again."

But she wasn't; for, by some miraculous means, concussion had stopped her lying. John left the hospital in a cloud of happiness—his beloved Meriam, her one imperfection gone, would be out of hospital in three days, although she was off work for a week.

They celebrated her return with a quiet dinner out.

"It's wonderful to have you back," he told her. "When will you marry me?"

"Whenever you like, John. I feel so much more sure of myself these days."

"And you'll come and meet my parents on Tuesday?"

"I'd love to, darling."

John Manners' father was a solicitor and lived in a neat little house at St Albans. The neatness came from his wife, a tidy little woman with a predilection for net curtains and high hedges, as though she and her husband held unspeakable orgies which must be kept from the other residents of Orchard Road; in fact, the nearest to orgiastic behaviour was a foursome at bridge on Saturday evenings.

Mrs Manners was aware that John had a girlfriend and wondered what defect she had that John never brought her to visit them. Now the great moment was approaching, for her son had made it clear that the girl he was bringing was her future daughter-in-law. She plumped up the cushions on the fawn sofa, and straightened one crooked duck flying across the wall; the table was set in the dining room and dinner neatly advanced in the kitchen. She smoothed the skirt of her new blue dress—wondering whether it wasn't perhaps too young for her—and walked over to the window to wait for the new arrivals.

John's old Ford was at the garage, so he and Meriam—"I wish you'd call me Mary, it *is* my real name"—travelled by train and managed to find a taxi at St Albans station.

"You are," said John, "still an invalid."

In the taxi Meriam clasped his hand.

"Do I look all right? I know blue suits me, but . . . and what will your mother think of my glasses? She'll think our children will all be short-sighted and she's probably right. . . ."

The taxi stopped and John helped Meriam out, paid the driver and held her arm as they went up the garden path and rang the door bell; John had a key but he felt the occasion demanded the formal ring.

Mrs Manners opened the door and drew them into the hall and, as they exchanged the banal comments of strangers who hope to become better acquainted, Mrs Manners was taking in the blue dress which reflected the colour of Meriam's eyes, the glasses which covered them, the way she did her hair, and the approximate cost of her shoes.

"Dinner will be in half an hour, but I expect you'd like a cup of tea in the meantime." She led the way to the living room. "This is my husband, James—I'll go and put the kettle on."

In no time she was back with a tea tray.

"We're having jugged hare for dinner—one of John's favourites—you do like jugged hare don't you, Meriam?"

"No, I'm afraid I don't."

Silence stretched as tea was poured out and handed round.

"I can make you an omelette," said Mrs Manners finally, and the matter appeared to be settled—and hopefully forgotten. Conversation returned safely to the weather, the garden and the wrong-headedness of the government. No one asked Meriam a direct question and all was peace until they stood up to go into dinner.

"New dress, mother?" asked John.

"Yes, do you like it? I'm not sure about the colour, and I'm afraid it might be a little young for me."

"No mother, it's perfect—isn't it, Meriam?"

Meriam of old would have assured his mother that it was perfect, that she was young enough and attractive enough to carry it off. Meriam of today thought for a moment.

"Well, truth to tell, blue isn't your colour, Mrs Manners, and I do think an older style would be more suitable."

Dinner was mainly a silent meal with John and his father commenting on cricket, football and golf about which neither knew much but both hoped that Meriam knew even less.

As soon as they had finished their coffee, which was served in the living room—and before anyone could misguidedly ask Meriam if she admired the flight of ducks—John said they must go and Mr Manners offered to drive them to the station.

During the drive he kept up a monologue on the high price of property—whether as a general subject or to dissuade John from marriage, with its subsequent acquisitions, his son was unable to divine.

John and Meriam parted on Meriam's doorstep. He kissed her lightly.

"Darling," he said, "I asked you to tell the truth, but not *all* the time."

The following day Meriam started work again, and when John called in the evening, he found her in tears.

"They were so horrible to me at the office," she wailed.

"What happened?"

"Shirley told us she'd got engaged to Brian Smith in accounts, and wasn't she lucky."

"And what did you say?" groaned John.

"The truth of course; that luck didn't come into it, as she'd worked so hard to hook him, and that he wasn't much of a catch because he's a fumbler—he almost got me in the stationery cupboard at the Christmas party."

"That was very unkind."

"It was the truth."

John wiped away her tears and one thing began to lead to another—which it hadn't since her concussion.

"Let's go over to the bed," he whispered in her ear.

She pulled herself free.

"Darling," she said, "there's a book I want you to look at first, and then we'll lie on the hearth-rug."

"Why?"

"The book says . . ." She reached out for it, and put it in his hand. "I'm going to change," she said.

He glanced at the book while she disappeared into the tiny bathroom. Anger mounted in him, and then she was back in a transparent black nightdress and draping herself on the rug. He threw the book in the corner and snatched off his jacket.

"Lie beside me," she said huskily.

"But why the book?"

"I thought it would be useful."

He knelt beside her.

"But you always said I made love superbly, that it was the most exciting . . ."

"I was a terrible liar."

He reached out his hand and grasped the poker which picturesquely hung by the gas fire. . . .

She looked very white as he took off her glasses, found a respectable housecoat and put it on her limp figure. Then he put on his jacket before dialling 999.

"Yes," he told the ambulancemen, "I'm afraid she wasn't wearing her glasses again and she hit her head on the fender."

THE STEEP DARK STAIRS

Ian Stuart

IT WAS ONE of those depressing late autumn afternoons when moisture drips from the bare trees and dusk comes early to city streets. I walked up the road from the Underground station without seeing a car pass in either direction; not much traffic came along Inkerman Road.

The houses were almost identical, three storeys high with steeply pitched slate roofs and heavy-silled bay windows, differing only in the colour of their faded paint. Outside Number 27 a faint mist clung round the street lamp as if for warmth. I inserted my key in the lock, turned it and pushed. The door opened with a slight creak. Next door at Number 29 a curtain moved at a downstairs window and a pale face hovered there. Then seeing that I had noticed it, withdrew again into the shadows.

"It's me, Mrs Wyatt," I called, stepping into the hall.

The old lady liked me to announce myself at once. She pretended it was to give her time to "make herself presentable", but I knew the truth was she was nervous. Afraid of some young thug breaking in and raping her. There was nothing to be ashamed of in that, she might be over eighty, but nowadays old age and infirmity were no defence against attack and robbery. If I were an old lady living alone, I'd have been nervous too.

"I'm in here, Mr Dalby." Her voice was still firm. No sign of enfeebled old age there.

As if I didn't know where she'd be, I thought. All the time I had been coming, she had never been anywhere but in the drawing room at the back of the house. Perhaps it was the weather, or the manager's keeping me late to discuss a routine return; Mr Hindley was a fussy little man obsessed with observing the letter of the rules and keeping out of trouble until he retired in two years time. Whatever it was, as I walked down Mrs Wyatt's tiled hall I felt a sudden spurt of irritation. It wasn't that I minded cashing a cheque for her once a week, I worked in the bank and it was no trouble, but I had been doing it for four years now, ever since Nora died, and this evening I wanted to get home.

My wife had taken to doing most of the old lady's shopping because Mrs Wyatt was nearly blind and there was a main road to cross to reach the shops and the local branch of the bank. Since Nora died I had cashed the weekly cheque and the home help the Council sent in twice a week did the shopping.

Ahead of me at the left of the hall the stairs rose steep and dark to the first-floor landing. Wide, straight stairs with heavy wooden banisters designed to accommodate Victorian pretensions and bulky Victorian skirts. Dangerous stairs for someone who was almost blind.

The drawing room was large and high-ceilinged but seemed smaller than it was because of the quantity of heavy old furniture crammed into it. Long velvet curtains hung at the french windows and a mirror in a mahogany frame over the tiled fireplace. Except where it was covered by the furniture, the pattern of the carpet had faded and worn until it was almost invisible, and there were some threadbare patches.

Mrs Wyatt was sitting in her favourite high-backed chair facing the television set. It was switched on, but she couldn't see the picture. Perhaps she listened to the sound. Or perhaps she exaggerated her blindness a little as old people sometimes do exaggerate their infirmities. Not that she made much of her bad heart, she hardly ever mentioned it.

"Any sudden shock and I could go just like that, so the doctor says," she had told me once in a rare moment of revelation. And she had laughed. She might not be a very nice old woman, but she had courage.

"Hello, Mrs Wyatt," I said. "I've brought your money." I took my wallet from my pocket and counted out the notes. "Forty pounds. I'll put it on the table under the ashtray."

What we said to each other hardly changed from week to week. That was where she liked me to leave the money, always forty pounds for the last year, weighted safely with a heavy glass ashtray she used only as a paperweight because she didn't smoke and she had few visitors. The first time I cashed her cheque for her I handed the money to her and she became quite flustered, scolding me as if I were a little boy instead of a man of 49 doing her a good turn. Holding it, I learnt, her hands weren't free to pick up her handbag from the floor beside her chair, and she didn't know what to do with it.

"Thank you, Mr Dalby."

We had lived next door to each other for over fifteen years, but anything less formal would have been unthinkable to us both. Once a week for four years, less a few when I was on holiday. She must have said that nearly two hundred times. Now the words came automatically, without thought, and I doubted if she really felt any gratitude. Like many old women, she took little services for granted, almost as her right.

"My nephew's coming to stay," she told me, a triumphant note in her voice.

"Oh?" I said. I could understand her excitement, it would be a major event for her. I couldn't remember anyone coming to stay here before.

"He's my only living relative. You might say, he's my heir." She cackled with laughter. "I've left something to the Blind, and the guide dogs, but the rest will go to Ronald. I've no one else to leave my bits and pieces to."

Bits and pieces! I thought. This house would realise at least £90,000 if it was sold now, probably a good deal more. That might not be a fortune, but it wouldn't be exactly a miserly inheritance for a nephew who had never visited his aunt before. And I knew she had some jewellery. Nothing really valuable, but nice Victorian pieces fetched good prices these days.

"That's the one who lives in Dembury?" I asked.

"Yes, Ronald. He's coming next Thursday."

"How long will he be here for?"

"I don't know. I hope he'll be able to stay a nice long time."

"Let's hope so." It was a lie, I didn't like the idea of his coming at all, and the longer he stayed the worse it would be.

"He's an accountant," Mrs Wyatt said. "He'll be able to advise me about my money."

"I'm sure he will," I agreed, a dreadful empty feeling at the pit of my stomach.

The nephew's name was Ronald Vickers. He was in his late thirties, a weedy man with a ridiculous little moustache and fair hair going thin on the top of his head. He looked weak and shifty, and I disliked him on sight.

Thursday was the day I cashed the old lady's cheque, and when I took her the money as usual on my way home he was there, sitting in one of the big easy chairs, his legs stretched out across the hearth-rug, very much at home. When she introduced him he didn't stand up to shake hands, he just nodded and gave me a complacent smirk. I didn't mind, it would make what I planned easier if I didn't like him.

"I'll leave my key, Mrs Wyatt," I said, ignoring him as pointedly as I could. "You won't need me to cash your cheque while Ron's here."

"Oh, Mr Dalby, I think I'd—" she began.

But Ron interrupted her. "That's right, we shan't," he agreed.

I put the key which originally she had given Nora on the table beside the forty pounds. He picked it up and started threading it on to his key-ring.

"Was there anything else?" he enquired rudely.

An expression of shock and disapproval flitted across his aunt's thin features. To her, bad manners were the exclusive privilege of the old, and she didn't like his usurping it. But she said nothing.

"No, nothing else," I replied.

I was glad to get out of the house.

The next day I started making enquiries about Ronald Vickers. Dembury wasn't a large town and by a lucky chance I knew a securities clerk in the bank there. I rang him and explained that Mrs Wyatt was an old customer and I didn't trust her nephew not to try to swindle her; I'd be glad if he could find out anything about him and let me know. He promised to see what he could do and ring me back.

He rang that afternoon. The nearest Vickers had ever come to being an accountant was a spell in the accounts department of a local firm when he was eighteen. They had sacked him. He was what he looked, a petty crook, and his speciality was conning old people out of their savings. He had been to prison three times, on the last occasion for eighteen months. The next time, I thought with satisfaction, it would be longer than eighteen months. A whole lot longer.

I told myself I must be patient and not rush things. It might look suspicious if anything happened too soon after his arrival.

The days passed and he showed no sign of leaving. I wondered what he had told his aunt to explain his not having to work. It was hardly likely he had confessed the truth, that he hadn't had a job since coming out of gaol the last time four months ago. Every evening just before nine he left the house and walked down the road, passing my window. It was a good hour before he returned and I suspected he visited The Bunch of Grapes, a big, brassy pub in the main road. It wasn't the sort of pub I liked, but one evening I looked in there about a quarter to ten, and sure enough he was in a corner of the saloon bar with a pinched looking middle aged blonde.

It occurred to me he might be an impostor, and not Ron Vickers at all. Mrs Wyatt hadn't seen her nephew for years, and nearly blind as she was, it probably wouldn't be too difficult to deceive her. At first when the idea struck me I nearly froze with panic. Then I saw it didn't make any difference. As far as I was concerned an imitation nephew was as good as the real thing. Better.

He had been there nearly a fortnight when one of the cashiers at the bank came to my desk and told me there was a customer at her till wanted to cash one of Mrs Wyatt's cheques.

"He says you know him and you'll say it's all right," she told me.

I looked up. It was Ron all right.

"Let me see the cheque," I told Jackie.

It was made out to "Cash" for two hundred pounds. Knowing Ron was watching me, I examined it carefully. The signature was almost certainly Mrs Wyatt's, he had probably persuaded her to sign it before he filled in the amount. Not that she would have been able to read what he'd written, anyway, but that sort of caution came naturally to crooks like him.

"I'll have a word with him," I said.

He appeared to be leaning on the counter casually, as if he hadn't a care in the world, but his eyes were wary and I could see he was nervous.

"Hello, Ron," I said.

"Hello, squire. What's the problem?"

"No problem."

"Auntie wants me to get her some things."

"That's all right," I told Jackie. "I know Mr Vickers."

Ron gave a sly grin and watched her count out the notes, stuffing them away in his wallet when she pushed them under the screen.

"Ugh!" she said when he had gone. "I didn't like him. I wouldn't trust him an inch."

"Neither would I," I agreed.

The more people who felt like that the better. Give him just a little more rope; I couldn't afford to wait much longer.

The next morning Hadley called me into his office. He was sitting at his desk, his forehead creased, looking more worried and harassed than ever.

"You know old Mrs Wyatt, don't you?" he asked.

"Yes," I agreed, wondering what was coming. My heart beat a little faster. "She lives next door to me."

"Is she all right?"

"How do you mean? She's nearly blind, and her heart isn't too strong—at least, she says it isn't—but she's all there. Is something wrong?" The pangs of anxiety were beginning to make themselves evident inside me.

"I've just had a call from her; she wants to give a nephew £4,000 to help him start some sort of business."

My anxiety evaporated. Ron must be desperate to risk queering his pitch by cashing the cheque yesterday and now trying to persuade her to "lend" him £4,000. Not that I minded, it would strengthen the evidence against him.

"It all sounds very unsatisfactory to me," Hadley went on. "She didn't even know what sort of business it was. 'A consultancy', she said!"

"He's a nasty bit of work," I told him. "But it's her money, I don't see there's much we can do about it if she's made up her mind."

"That's just the point," Hadley said miserably. "It isn't, she hasn't got anything like £4,000. Not here, anyhow. There's less than a hundred in her cheque account and fifty-seven pounds in her savings account."

"Oh," I said.

"She used to keep good balances. I've looked. Three years ago she had nearly £3,000 on her cheque account, but she's run it right down. You know what some of these old people are, they don't realize how expensive everything's become and they can't go on living like they used to. It looks as if she spends quite a lot from the run of her account."

"I saw she was getting a bit low the other day," I admitted. "And her nephew cashed a cheque of hers for £200 yesterday."

"Has she any other money, do you know?" Hadley asked. "Investments or anything?"

"Not as far as I know."

He looked more worried than ever. "Do you think the nephew's been putting pressure on her?"

It was exactly what I did think. Old people, especially lonely old women like Mrs Wyatt, were very vulnerable to undue influence. And it was difficult to prove.

"I wouldn't be surprised," I said.

"Oh lord! I'd better ring her back and try to explain," Hadley said miserably. It wasn't pleasant telling somebody one of their nearest and dearest was robbing them. Often they took their hurt and wounded pride out on you.

"I could slip round to see her this evening," I volunteered. "She trusts me."

"Would you?" His eagerness was pathetic. Then his face fell. "But if he's there . . ."

"He won't be. He goes out to the pub every evening."

"I'll leave it to you then, Harry. That would be the best way."

Hadley looked so pleased with himself you'd have thought he was the one who was taking the responsibility.

Sitting in the darkness of my front room, the curtains not quite closed, I waited impatiently for Ron to depart for The Bunch of Grapes. The minutes dragged by. I hardly ever used that room and the air felt cold and damp, but I didn't dare to fetch an electric fire in case he came out while I was away.

Nine o'clock passed and he still hadn't appeared. Then, at four minutes past, when I was beginning to wonder if he was going out this evening after all, I heard the front door of

Number 27 close and he came down the few feet of path to the road, walking with his curious, furtive gait.

I closed the curtains and went along the hall to my kitchen. The few things I needed were lying ready on the table. What I planned wouldn't take long, but I couldn't afford the time to search for them, I must be back here in my own house before Ron returned. Ticking them off mentally as I did so, I slipped them into my jacket pocket one by one: a length of thin cord about seven feet long, a penknife and a torch. Satisfied, I left the house by the front door, leaving on the hall light.

It was a mild evening, but I shivered convulsively as I walked up the path of Number 27. For a second or two my resolution faltered and I had to fight an impulse to turn back. But there could be no retreating now, that way lay ruin and, a distinct possibility, prison. Taking from my pocket the key I had had cut before returning the original to Mrs Wyatt, I pushed it into the lock and turned it. The door opened with its familiar little creak. I stepped into the hall and closed the door behind me.

An edge of light was showing under the drawing room door and I could hear the television or radio on in there. From the roars of laughter it sounded like a variety show. The light seemed to accentuate the darkness in the hall and I could see nothing of the stairs just ahead and to my left. It wasn't fear of being discovered there that set my nerves on edge and my heart thudding, Ron wouldn't be back for an hour at least, and if the old lady came out, she wouldn't see me, it was the prospect of what I was going to do. Murder was irrevocable.

My conscience wasn't troubling me. In a detached sort of way I was sorry about Mrs Wyatt, but while she lived I was in danger. Killing her was necessary. It was a question of self-defence. Anyway, she was old, and she didn't have much of a life blind and with a weak heart. As for Ron, it was only poetic justice he should be blamed for her death, he was a crook and he had been swindling her. Moreover, if it hadn't been for his coming here there would have been no need for his aunt to die, things could have gone on as they had for the last four years. I'd got it all worked out.

I edged forward. How much farther? Ten feet? Twelve? The darkness was almost tangible, something solid I could feel. But perhaps that was nerves too.

My right foot stumbled against something. Panic gripped me. Whatever it was was soft and yielding. A cat? Mrs Wyatt disliked cats, but an inquisitive animal might have smuggled itself into the house for warmth. No, it couldn't be. A cat would have sensed my coming, and streaked off, screeching, when I kicked it. This thing hadn't moved, and it was too heavy for a cat.

I had to use my torch now. Hands trembling, I took it from my pocket, wrapped my left hand round the glass to mask the light, and switched it on. There, lying in a heap at the foot of the stairs, her skirt dragged up and her right leg trailing across the bottom tread, was Mrs Wyatt.

For a moment I was too startled to move. Shock had drained all the strength from my limbs. Then the moment passed. I made myself stoop down and feel for the pulse in her neck. There was nothing. The old woman was dead.

I find it hard now to remember what I felt at that moment. Shock, yes. But most, I think, relief. Mrs Wyatt was dead, and I had played no part in her death. She must have gone upstairs after Ron went out, tripped and fallen. All my planning, all my fear had been unnecessary. Now all I had to do was get home as quickly as possible, leaving Ron to find her when he returned.

I retraced the few steps to the door, switched off my torch and let myself out. A minute later I was safely back in my own house.

It was just after eleven the next morning when the two men came to the bank and asked to see Hadley. After they had been with him about ten minutes he rang through and asked me to go in.

"This is Detective Superintendent Haynes," he told me, introducing the elder of the two. "And Detective Sergeant Clark."

I felt a spasm of apprehension. But what had I to be afraid of? Intending to commit a murder wasn't a crime, and I hadn't been responsible for Mrs Wyatt's death. Anyway, they couldn't be here about that, a fatal fall downstairs wouldn't involve a superintendent. It must be something else. I felt their eyes on me, sizing me up.

"It's about old Mrs Wyatt," Hadley explained.

"Oh?" I hoped I had achieved the right blend of interest and surprise.

"She was found dead in her house this morning," the Superintendent said.

"Oh, I'm sorry. She was over eighty, and I know her heart wasn't too strong."

"It wasn't her heart. She fell down the stairs."

"Oh no!" I really did sound shocked, I thought. "They're very steep and she was almost blind."

"So we understand."

"It must have been a shock for Ron, finding her."

"Ron? Mr Vickers, you mean?"

"Yes. He's her nephew, he's staying with her." But they know that, I told myself.

"He didn't find her."

"Oh?" I was startled. "Who did?"

"The home help, a lady called Mrs Price. Mr Vickers stayed with a friend last night." Haynes paused. "When did *you* last see the old lady, Mr Dalby?"

"Several days ago."

"You're sure of that?"

"Yes."

"Didn't you go to see her last night?" Hadley asked, looking puzzled. "You said you would."

"I tried, but there wasn't any answer," I told him.

"Something to do with her account?" the Superintendent enquired.

Hadley nodded. To me he said, "Head Office have agreed that in the circumstances we may provide the police with any information they want."

"Circumstances?" I repeated.

"We're not satisfied Mrs Wyatt's death was an accident," Haynes explained. "She died some time yesterday evening, but the light wasn't on, and it looks as if she tripped over a cord that had been tied across one of the top stairs. It had broken, but the ends were still there. She fell backwards down the stairs and broke her neck." He turned to Hadley. "Why was Mr Dalby going to see her last night, sir?"

There were two police cars outside Number 27 when I returned in at my gate that evening. I wondered if they had arrested Ron yet. He must have fastened the cord across the stairs before he went off to the pub to meet his friend. The pinched looking blonde, I supposed. Perhaps even now he was, in the time-honoured phrase, helping the police with their enquiries.

As I took my key-ring from my pocket I felt like singing. I was safe. Nobody would know now what I had done. Good old Ron, he had no idea what a good turn he had done me last night.

I tried to push the key into the lock. Only the first quarter of an inch or so went in. I took it out and studied it.

"Is it the wrong key, Mr Dalby?"

I turned. Haynes was standing by the gate, two other men just behind him.

"May I see it?" he asked pleasantly.

"It's an old key," I muttered. Even to me my voice sounded strange. "I had to change the lock."

"Oh?" Haynes was still holding out his hand. There was nothing I could do but give him the key. "It doesn't look old," he said. "Robinson?"

A uniformed constable stepped forward and took it. With a dreadful sense of the inevitable, I watched him walk up the next door path, insert the key in the lock and turn it. The door opened.

Why hadn't I got rid of it this morning? I thought, angered by my own stupidity. But I knew why, I had been so sure I had nothing to fear. And I still hadn't. If Ron said he had seen me return the key his aunt had given me it would be his word against mine, and he was not only a suspect with a motive, he was a crook with a police record.

"Not your old key then, Mr Dalby?" Haynes said.

"I must have mixed them up. I thought I'd given hers back to Mrs Wyatt, but I can't have done."

"Perhaps you meant to—at the time. Mr Vickers tells us his aunt asked you for it but you didn't give it to her. He says she remarked only yesterday that she must ask you for it again now he was living there and could cash her cheques for her."

I was shocked and angry. How could Ron lie like that? Why should he? But I knew why.

"He's lying," I said desperately.

"Very likely," Haynes agreed. "I wouldn't think he's a man who's what you might call particular about the truth. But it doesn't make any difference, does it, Mr Dalby? Either you kept the key, or you had a duplicate cut before you returned it to Mrs Wyatt." He paused. "Shall we go inside? I daresay the neighbours are watching and wondering what's going on."

Inside, the house was cold and unwelcoming. In silence I led the way into the dining room. The other men came too; one of them stationed himself by the window, the other stayed just inside the door.

"She was a very methodical old lady," the Superintendent observed. "And she wasn't quite as blind as she pretended. That's why it seemed strange there were no bank statements in the drawer with her other papers. Receipts, cheque books, cheque stubs, everything else, but no statements. Not for the last four years. And the counterfoils were all filled in. Only there weren't any amounts for the cheques she'd made payable to 'Cash'. Funny that."

"I made out those cheques," I said. My mouth was dry. "She asked me to, and there didn't seem any need to fill in the amount, she had seventy pounds every week."

"You're sure that's what you gave her? Seventy pounds?"

"Yes, of course I am."

"It seems rather a lot of cash for an old lady living alone who hardly ever went out. Especially as she seems to have paid most of her bills by cheque. Don't you think so?"

"I suppose it does," I agreed. "But that's what she wanted."

"And you used to bring her her statement, it was never posted to her. That's what they told me at the bank."

"I explained it to her."

"Yes, of course. She couldn't see well enough to read, could she? One of her neighbours says the old lady told her you looked after all her business affairs for her. Only she said you cashed forty pounds for her every week. Forty, not seventy, Mr Dalby." Haynes paused. "What happened when you went to see her last night?"

"Nothing. I couldn't make her hear. She must have had the television on. You heard me tell Mr Hadley this morning."

"So I did. But another neighbour says she saw you let

yourself in. She knew you had a key, and as it was you she wasn't worried, but she did think it was a funny time for you to be going to see the old lady."

"All right," I said. "I did let myself in. But she was dead. Ron did it. He's a crook, he's been to gaol. And he was her heir."

"We know all about Mr Vickers," Haynes told me. "He's been very frank. He says she told him she was leaving most of her money to charities for the blind and it would have suited him better for her to stay alive. That way he could have talked her into giving him money now and again."

"He's lying!" I shouted. "She never told him that. He thought he was getting all her money. That's why he killed her."

"But he had an alibi. You hadn't," Haynes pointed out.

"A phoney one. Can't you see that? He's a crook!"

"And you aren't, you're respectable. You were scared he'd find out what you'd been up to all these years and tell her. I reckon it must come to around £6,000 you swindled her out of. It would have been the end for you, wouldn't it? You'd have lost your job and your pension, and probably gone to prison. Now there's a chance you'll go anyway."

I was almost weeping. "I tell you she was dead when I got there!" I cried.

It was the truth, but nobody believed me.

THE DOCTOR AFRAID OF BLOOD

Herbert Harris

AT THE MOMENT when Dr Gordon's eyes first wandered, by some providential chance, to that scarlet fingerprint, the shock was so sudden, so intense, that it made him feel momentarily sick.

He realized uneasily that the colour had drained from his face, that his hands were trembling uncontrollably. "Jesus," he thought, "I mustn't let them see that I'm afraid."

The ghastly, seemingly endless interview was nearly over. Perhaps, after all, the men from the C.I.D. would go away without ever having noticed that scarlet print. But this was merely wishful thinking, wasn't it? They would go on examining minutely every inch of the woman's flat to make absolutely sure they had missed nothing of importance.

Fortunately the tell-tale fingerprint—*his*, of course—was slightly in shadow. Some pink carnations in a vase—quite dead now, like the pink and blonde fashion model Sandra—stood between that blood-red fingerprint and the light from the window.

"Dr Gordon. . . ."—Detective Inspector Matthews had turned slowly to address him again—"you were the last person, as far as we know, to call on Sandra Lake. In your professional capacity, of course." (Was there just a hint of cynicism in the way he said that?) "Is everything in this flat exactly as it was when you last called here . . . ?"

The doctor nervously ran a tongue over dry lips. "Yes, I suppose so. I'm not really sure. Why?"

"Naturally, Doctor, we are anxious to establish if she had any visitors yesterday. So far we seem to have drawn a blank."

Dr Gordon was aware that beads of sweat had formed at his temples. He said, "Well, we know she must have had at least one visitor, Inspector—the man who killed her, if it was a man, of course."

Inspector Matthews just stood there in the middle of the room, saying nothing, looking at nothing in particular. Why the hell couldn't he call it a day and go away, Dr Gordon thought. But he had begun to think the C.I.D. men would never go.

He cast another brief and frightened glance at the red fingerprint, half hoping it had disappeared or would somehow vanish soon, but he knew it couldn't. Whose fingerprint could it be but his own? And if one of them chanced to notice it. . . .

Oh God, one more meticulous examination of this room, and they couldn't miss it. It was near the edge of that small occasional table. If the table had only been, say, dark oak, the print would not have mattered, it would not have shown. But the table was painted a pale cream, making the bloody print stand out like a red light . . . to the frightened doctor, at least.

It was ludicrous really. One tiny oval of blood making *him*, a hardened medico, tremble at the knees, break out in a clammy sweat. But that tiny patch of blood, made undoubtedly by one of his fingers touching the table, could mean the end of everything.

Sandra would have laughed if she could have seen him now. Perhaps she would have said in her mocking Marilyn Monroe voice, "Poor darling . . . gweat big doctor fwightened by teeny-weeny patch of blood!"

She had laughed too often and too long. And when the original physical appeal had begun to wear thin, he had quite brutally told her so. Until then he had been afraid only of her body, the way it had enslaved him, diminished him.

Now, suddenly, he was afraid of her vindictive mind. "You don't imagine you can get rid of me? Do you want me to get you struck off, darling? Scandalous conduct with a female patient and all that? It would be so simple . . . with you on drugs, too. . . ."

He couldn't be absolutely sure, but he thought she had smiled that taunting smile even when she died—at the moment when, overwhelmed by that insensate rage he had never been able to control, he had plunged that stiletto-like letter opener once, twice, three times into her body.

The memory of it added further torture to his tortured mind. But they couldn't possibly suspect *him*, could they? He was too well respected as a doctor, surely? . . . a man who took an active part in community affairs, on the local council, the committee of the youth club. A man like Dr Gordon didn't go around stabbing blonde models to death. It was utterly out of character. So how could they . . . ?

No, they had nothing to go on except that tiny imprint of blood near the edge of the cream table. . . . *his* fingerprint. He had treated the girl for migraine, and they would find it hard to believe if he told them that *her* blood had got on to *his* hand for purely professional reasons. In any case, it was unlikely *her* blood matched his own rare blood group. . . .

So he must think of something . . . think, man, think!

Suddenly he was feeling in his jacket pockets with his sweating, still shaking hands. He smiled faintly at Inspector Matthews.

"You wouldn't have a cigarette, old chap?"

Looking surprised, the detective produced a packet. Dr Gordon took a cigarette, felt again in his pockets, and said: "I'm afraid I haven't a light either—just the habit!"

The Inspector obligingly produced a lighter and lit his cigarette. Dr Gordon immediately turned away, puffing hard, and strolled casually over to where the small table stood—the small cream-painted table near the edge of which was that imprint of his finger made with Sandra's too-warm blood. . . .

Controlling the tremor in his voice, he said: "Miss Lake kept a lot of letters in that small writing-desk in the corner, Inspector. I suppose you've thought of looking in there?"

"It was almost the first place we looked, Doctor."

"Yes . . . yes, of course, it would be. Only I was just wondering. . . . "

With a show of distraction, he put the glowing cigarette down on the small cream table, its tip projecting over the edge by just a fraction.

Wondering what, Doctor?"

Gordon strolled over to the writing desk. "I seem to recall her using some kind of secret drawer on one occasion, but I may have imagined it. If I could only remember. . . . "

He lowered the front of the desk, pretending to study its

interior. He hoped, as he played for time, that the Inspector would be studying *him*. I'm smarter than they are, he thought. Just a question of distracting their attention for a while so that they wouldn't notice that burning cigarette doing its work.

He had placed the cigarette with great care in what he estimated was exactly the right spot.

Soon, he calculated, the cigarette would start to burn the cream paint. Christ, they mustn't notice the smell. He would have to keep their attention occupied in some way. They mustn't catch sight of that cigarette until it had burned its way right through the middle of that tiny red oval, scorching the fingerprint into an unrecognizable state. . . .

Inspector Matthews was glancing over his shoulder, and the Doctor, licking the sweat from his upper lip, said with a wry smile: "No, Inspector, no secret drawer. Just my imagination. But you had a look at everything in the desk, I suppose? One of my bills here, I see. She was a private patient. And quite a few letters. . . . " (and the cruel-looking letter opener, wiped clean.)

"Yes, we've seen all those, Doctor. They're all from women oddly enough. Did she show any lesbian tendencies?"

"Good heavens, no!" (That was a damned silly thing to say, a bad mistake.) "I mean, there were never any signs." The C.I.D. man was studying him disconcertingly, saying nothing. "No men friends? That's rather odd, Inspector, isn't it? Miss Lake was an extremely attractive woman."

"Yes, very."

"I should have thought men would have swarmed round her."

He knew, of course, that Sandra had never been promiscuous. He had been the only one she had really fastened on to. Like a limpet. That had been her undoing. A pity there had *not* been a few other men in her life. This would have given the C.I.D. ferrets something else to get their teeth into, some other suspects to follow around. . . .

He just had to keep them occupied while the cigarette burned its way through that red fingerprint. Only a minute longer perhaps. . . .

But the Inspector turned away suddenly, and Dr Gordon

watched in agony of apprehension as he moved across to the small cream table and picked up the cigarette.

"You really should be more careful where you put down your cigarettes, Doctor." The C.I.D. man stubbed it out in an ashtray. "You've started to burn a groove in the table."

"Have I? Oh, dear . . . careless of me!" He could feel his heart hammering against his ribs, the perspiration trickling down under his shirt.

"I understood you didn't smoke, Doctor. Haven't you been warning the members of the youth club against smoking, condemning cigarette smoking in the local papers?"

"Yes, you're quite right, Inspector. But I . . . I very occasionally get an urge . . . like just now. . . ."

"To soothe your nerves, I expect," Inspector Matthews said pointedly. "I did notice how badly your hands were shaking. I was wondering, in fact, if you were going to be able to put that cigarette down in the right spot."

"The right spot?"

"On this fingerprint, Doctor. It wasn't a bad effort. Full marks for trying. Another minute or two and it would have been scorched beyond recognition. I suppose I *could* have saved you all that trouble by mentioning the print earlier. . . ."

The Inspector broke off, eyeing Gordon with an expression mingling pity and contempt. He felt a little sorry for the doctor. He had never enjoyed watching a man go to pieces. And Gordon had crumpled badly, collapsing into a chair, hiding his face behind long sensitive fingers.

"We think we know how that print got there, Doctor. What's your version?"

Gordon tried desperately to say something coherent, but only a sort of gibberish emerged from his lips. He wanted to sob, to be sick. In his mind's eye he saw himself sitting beside that table after he had suffered the brainstorm and killed her— sitting there in a sort of trance and pouring himself a drink from her bottle of whisky. That was when he must have touched the edge of the table. . . .

He had wiped everything clean, everything, he realised now, except that table. Strange how he had noticed that tiny red patch today for the first time, but not when he had put it there. . . .

Inspector Matthews and Sergeant Dawson were staring down at him. Like executioners. Their eyes boring into his soul. He looked up. "I'll . . . I'll tell you what happened."

When at last he had finished speaking, the Inspector said: "I'm glad you decided to get it off your chest, Doctor. Always the best thing. But in case you should wonder why I didn't mention that fingerprint before, I'd better tell you that the print is not yours."

Gordon raised his head slowly, blinking. "Not mine?"

"No. The fingerprint was left by Sandra Lake herself . . . some time before you killed her, Doctor. And it wasn't even blood. It was a red shoe-cream that she used for cleaning some red shoes."

Dr Gordon buried his face in his hands again, but presently began laughing—laughter that began quietly and grew into hysteria. Somewhere . . . somewhere . . . Sandra would be laughing too in her specially derisive way.

THE DEAD DON'T STEAL

Ella Griffiths

THE RINGING OF the phone on his desk brought Curt Lessner's head up with a jerk. Every time it rang he was afraid it was the police.

This time it was—the Traffic Division.

"'Morning, Mr Lessner," a friendly Bergen voice said. "Inspector Svendsen here. We've found your car. At least, our friends across the border have. Found it in Arvika—double-parked outside a supermarket. Double-parked and with a lady's handbag on the seat. Full of the usual junk, you know—powder compact, comb, all that sort of stuff. Driving licence, too. *And* a couple of credit cards. Shouldn't take long to trace who owns it. One of my lads is on to it now."

A feeble "Oh?" was all Lessner was able to manage before the inspector went on: "The Swedes drove your car to the border and we picked it up there. The forensic boys'll have to give it a good going-over first—prints, you know, things like that—then you can have it back. It's all in one piece, so don't worry."

"Well, thank you," Curt Lessner said, clearing his throat. "Strange that someone should leave a handbag in it, though, isn't it?" he ventured.

"The woman who took your car did more than leave her bag behind," Inspector Svendsen answered. "On the way to Arvika she stopped at a café. 'Anders'', it's called. Just the other side of the border. Had a snack. Well, a dinner, actually. Meat and veg and all the trimmings. Anyway, somehow she managed to break a sauceboat. Sauce all over the place, the manager said. Most of it went on to the sofa, I gather. Nothing on *her*, apparently. The manager took it in his stride, but she was awfully put out, it seems—wanted to pay for the damage and getting the sofa cleaned. In the end she left her card so's they could contact her when they knew what it came to. So there you are: we've had it handed to us on a plate, so to speak." The Inspector laughed heartily at his own joke.

"But how'd you find all this out so quickly?" Lessner asked. "That she'd stopped at a café, I mean."

"Simple. The bill from 'Anders'' was in her bag. Dated the same day. The Swedish police checked with the café, and there you are."

"But if you know that much, then you must know her name as well. I mean to say, driving licence and all that. . . . "

"Of course we do," the policeman agreed. "It's no secret. Lillen Aas. Lillen Johanne Aas, to be exact. Lives in Skippergaten, out at Nordstrand. Number twenty-two. Three-roomed flat. Very nice too, I hear. Not my department, actually, but I sent one of our cars up to have a look. There was no one home. Never mind, she's bound to turn up soon. And when she does we'll let you know."

"Lillen Aas?" Curt Lessner stammered. "But she's my secretary! She's been off work for a few days—since Monday, in fact. But it's only been two days since my car disappeared. . . . "

"Nothing very strange about that," said the Inspector. "She could have taken your car without showing up for work, couldn't she? Did you ever lend it to her, by the way?"

"Yes, sometimes. Odd errands for the office, you know."

"Will you be wanting to take the matter further, Mr Lessner?" the Inspector asked. "Prosecute, that is."

"Er, er . . . I don't know." Lessner made an effort to pull himself together. "I suppose I ought to, really. But Lillen . . . Do I have to decide that now?" he asked.

"No, Mr Lessner," the inspector reassured him. "There's plenty of time for that."

Curt Lessner thanked him and put the phone down. His mind reeling, he buried his face in his hands. Lillen—Lill— couldn't possibly have stolen his car. Nor could she have broken a sauceboat in a café in Sweden.

People who're dead don't steal cars. They don't steal anything.

And Lillen Aas *was* dead.

He'd killed her himself.

Everything had gone so well until Lill entered his life.

Blonde, petite, with eyes of speedwell blue, one day she had walked blithely into his office to apply for the vacant post of secretary in the small charter business and travel agency he had opened a bare three years earlier.

"I haven't many references, I'm afraid," she'd said with a disarming smile. "On the other hand I learn fast."

She was twenty-six. A woman, but a woman who, outwardly at least, had somehow retained the naïveté of a child.

"Can you type?"

"Yes. Not all that fast, but I'm pretty accurate. I have it taped, in other words."

"'Taped'?" he'd mused. Strange expression for a girl as young as she was to use.

Later he'd come to realize that she was full of contradictions like that.

She was right about learning fast.

She did. Very fast.

Annie hadn't liked her at all—understandably. Having been married to her Curt for twenty-odd years, she soon tumbled to it that he was up to something. Or, rather, that *they* were. And she'd been correct. Only three nights later he and his new secretary found themselves in bed together.

After that there was no going back, at least not for him.

He'd misjudged her completely. Taken it for granted that she'd jump at a chance to get into the racket. Earn a small fortune and then perhaps in a few years, when they'd stashed enough away, decamp to the Caribbean. Both of them. Settle down and enjoy life in a country where prices were more reasonable than in Norway and where a person could bask in sunshine all year round instead of spending half the time frozen to the marrow. The plan was simplicity itself. All she had to do was to act as a courier. Take parties of tourists over, show them around, and bring them back. Only in her luggage on the return trip there was always a wad or two of brightly coloured tourist brochures, tightly held by elastic bands. Nothing strange about that. If she were ever asked, she had only to say that they needed them to help make brochures of their own in Norwegian. But she never *was* asked—which was just as well, as a small space cut out in the middle of each bundle was packed tight with cocaine.

After three trips Lill had suddenly called a halt. She wanted out. She'd earned enough to make her comfortable, and added to that she'd fallen for one of the pilots on the Rio run. So that was that.

"But what about me?" he'd protested, his whole world suddenly shattered.

"You? You'll be all right. You're not exactly short of money, are you? And as for you-know-what, well—you have your Annie. You *are* married, you know. Besides, you're twenty years older than I am, don't forget. Twenty. That's eighteen too many as far as I'm concerned."

If only she'd not brought up the difference in their ages! Or not smiled so . . . condescendingly. Pityingly, almost. She'd made him feel practically senile.

That was why he'd killed her. Not that he'd meant to.

Before he realized it he'd lashed out at her and caught her a glancing blow behind the ear with the flat of his hand. It had sent her reeling, and as she fell her head struck the corner of his desk with a dull thud. Even now he wasn't sure whether it was he or the desk that had killed her. What he did know was that she was undeniably dead. She'd just crumpled to the floor and lain staring up at him with sightless blue eyes until finally, unable to bear it any longer, he'd steeled himself to close them.

Aghast at what he'd done, he'd sat down for a moment to consider his next move. Strangely enough, there didn't seem to be any blood, and it was that which had encouraged him to try to get away with it. The point was: how?

Obviously he had to get the body out of his office without being seen. Now, right away. It was already getting late—which fortunately meant that it was dark.

That was probably why he'd managed it.

But *had* he managed it? It was all beginning to seem unreal.

After the Inspector's phone call he sat quietly for a while, trying to steady his nerves. Then he locked up the office and drove home in the car he'd hired in place of his own. As soon as he got in he strode across to the drinks cabinet in the living room and poured himself a stiff measure of whisky. Gulping it down almost in one, he seated himself at the window and stared out into the night.

Before him lay the garden, but all he saw was the place where Lill's body lay, deep in some undergrowth, well off the beaten track.

"What's wrong, Curt?" his wife asked sharply, entering the room from the kitchen. "You've been acting so strangely lately. What's got into you?"

"The police phoned," he answered, his face averted. "Just before I left. They've found the car. Across the border in Arvika. Lillen's handbag was on the seat. There were some other things, too—"

"That hussy!" his wife burst out. "A hussy and a thief, that's what she is! It doesn't surprise me in the least. I've known it all along. Well, it'll put a stop to your fun and games, that's one good thing."

"Don't talk like that, Annie," her husband said thickly. "There's never been anything between us. I've told you so before. All I've ever done is to defend her when you kept on running her down. Anyway, I don't think *she* took the car. More likely someone else who wanted to hurt her for some reason."

"There you go again, defending her! If she didn't steal the car, why hasn't she shown a sign of life? Reported her handbag missing. She's bound to have had something in it more important than a compact and a lipstick. Women always do these days. Credit cards, that kind of thing. Oh, no, this time she's gone too far! Just wait till I see her again, I'll tell her a thing or two, believe you me! She can't twist *me* round her little finger, the way she can you."

Curt Lessner looked at his wife without answering. Suddenly he rose to his feet and stumbled to the bathroom. He reached it just in time to be sick into the wash-basin.

He knew Lill was dead. And the dead don't steal.

Later that night he was taken really ill. He felt feverish and several times he found himself in the bathroom again, trying to

be sick. Only now the sole result was a heaving stomach and a
dry rasp in his throat.

"You can't go on like this, Curt," his wife said. "We shall
have to get the doctor." They were the first kind words she'd
spoken to him for a long time, he reflected sadly. Ever since
Lillen Aas had come into his life, in fact.

"It'll pass," he assured her. "I'll be all right in the morning,
you'll see. I must have had something that's disagreed with
me."

His wife gave him a searching look but held her peace.

As he lay tossing and turning, unable to sleep, he realized
that she too was still awake. His brain was in a whirl. What on
earth was he to do? He was certain that Lill was dead. But
dead people don't steal cars, he reasoned yet again. Or spill
sauce on sofas. . . .

Shortly before nine next morning he phoned the inspector
and told him—which was true enough—that he thought the
whole story of the car theft had something fishy about it. "Why
should she leave her bag on the seat?" he asked. "And how
did she come to break a sauceboat? Sounds crazy to me. Do
you have a description of her? The people at the café must
remember what she looked like."

"All I know is that she was blonde and looked very young.
Childlike, the manager said. But I can phone the police in
Arvika and ask if they know any more, if you like," the
policeman offered.

"No, don't bother," Curt Lessner said hastily. "There's no
need for that. It's just that it all seems so strange to me. I
mean, she only had to ask me and I'd have let her have the car
anyway. She must have known that—"

"Just a moment," the Inspector broke in. "Hang on a sec,
will you?" Curt Lessner heard him lay the receiver aside and
walk away. When, a minute or so later, he returned, the
Inspector said: "It seems that the car was full of Lillen Johanne
Aas's fingerprints. So there we are—it must have been her
who drove it to Arvika."

"Oh, well—yes, I see. That settles it, then, doesn't it?"
Lessner said lamely, hurrying to replace the receiver before it
fell from his hand.

While he was shaving he studied his face in the mirror.

"God," he thought to himself, "I look like death warmed up."
He shuddered as the grotesque aptness of the expression
suddenly struck him. At breakfast he gave up after a tentative
bite of toast.

"Stay at home, Curt," his wife urged him. "You can't go to
the office in that state. It's Saturday, anyway. And I'd be a
darned sight happier if you'd let the doctor have a look at
you."

"Nonsense," her husband replied irritably. "Of course I'm
going. Place doesn't run itself, you know."

He changed his mind, however, when he realized that
Annie was going into town. If he really had been having
hallucinations, he'd better find out straightaway. And the only
way to do that was to go back to where he'd hidden Lill's body
and make sure.

If only none of it had ever happened! "Oh, God," he
thought to himself, "let it all be in my mind!" But somehow he
knew that it wasn't.

He felt he would give anything to be able to see Lill again.
Just to see her—alive! She could marry anyone she liked. He'd
never trouble her again. No other woman, either. He'd learnt
his lesson. Dear, dear Lill . . . .

As soon as his wife was safely out of the house he took the
hire car and drove the same route he'd taken on that fateful
night with Lill's body lying crumpled up under a blanket on
the back seat. Her last drive. It *must* have been.

He stopped the car at the same place as last time. Nerving
himself, he opened the door and half walked, half ran to the
thicket into which he had thrust the body.

Stumbling into the midst of it, he parted the bushes and
peered into the shadows. The body was exactly where he had
left it.

At that moment he heard the sound of footsteps crashing
through the bushes behind him.

It was the police.

First to arrive on the scene was Inspector Svendsen, the
policeman he'd spoken to on the phone. Just behind, Curt
Lessner glimpsed the trim figure of a woman. The inspector
introduced her: Detective Sergeant Sylvia Larsgaard.

"I realized as soon as Lill disappeared that something serious must have happened to her. She loved that flat of hers. It was almost a part of her. She'd never have gone off and left it like that. She told me once that she knew something about you that could ruin you for life, only she never said what it was. As the days went by, I got to thinking about what she'd said. That's what made me take your car. I thought that if you'd killed her and I could fix it so that it seemed she was still alive—well, with a bit of luck you'd feel you had to go back and see. She had the other key, remember? I found it on her dressing-table. And—well, it worked, didn't it?"

Detective Sergeant Sylvia Larsgaard. Blonde, petite, eyes like speedwells. Four or five years older than Lill, but even so the very image of her sister.

THE LAST OF THE MIDNIGHT GARDENERS

Tony Wilmot

WALTER OATES SAID: "That's the third midnight gardener this week." He threw the typescript into his out-tray and yawned. "Do we have any appointments this afternoon, Edna?"

Miss Tewsland, his secretary, smiled; she wasn't quite sure what he meant, but she had learned that if anything was guaranteed to exasperate a fiction editor it was contributors who sent in stories involving the type of characters Mr Oates called "midnight gardeners".

She checked the appointments book. "None . . . Walter," she cooed.

Walter nodded, pleased. Edna always showed plenty of leg whenever she leaned across her desk; it was one of the things he liked about her.

"Well, then, why don't we take the afternoon off. I know a cosy little bistro in Soho. . . . "

The phone rang. Miss Tewsland answered it and handed him the receiver, mouthing: "Your wife."

Walter said: "Hello, dear. Yes, it *is* rather a busy time right now. No, dear, I don't know what time I'll be home." He caught the expression in Miss Tewsland's eyes. "But I expect I'll be late."

Walter hung up and winked at Miss Tewsland; he was looking forward to a leisurely lunch. And afterwards . . . well, Miss Tewsland's flat was only a taxi-ride from the bistro . . . and she was always the soul of discretion.

At his club next day Walter was buttonholed by his barrister friend, Reggie. "We need your professional opinion, old boy. About the *modus operandi* of murder."

Groaning inwardly, Walter joined Reggie's group; he would much rather be thinking about Edna.

"We were saying, Walter, how so many wife murderers are mild-mannered, insignificant little chaps. But I don't suppose the fellows who write for your crime magazine bother about that. I bet their murderers have more than a touch of James Bond. Am I right?"

"Sorry to disappoint you, Reggie. The characters are just like the creators. They're all bank clerks, civil servants, insurance men. . . .

"They live in suburbia and suffer in silence for years. Then one day something snaps. They do in the wife and bury her in the cabbage patch—usually in the middle of the night. Ridiculous, of course. Which is why I call them midnight gardeners. Police would rumble them in ten seconds flat."

Over a brandy Reggie said: "Well then, there's an idea for your magazine, Walter. A competition for the perfect murder—told in story form. The rules would be simple: no psychopaths, no crimes of passion, no killing in self defence.

"It must be murder premeditated. With a logical motive. And it must be foolproof, so that even if the police suspected, they'd never be able to prove it."

Jane, Walter's wife, said: "You ought to relax more. Bringing all that work home."

Walter merely grunted. Since the announcement of the competition, entries had been pouring in. But none even came close to being feasible *and* foolproof. Too many weed killers, barbiturate overdoses, electric shocks in the bath.

"What about that one, dear . . . a man uses a blade of ice as a knife."

"Old hat," Walter snapped. Jane had never taken any real interest in crime stories; nurse-and-doctor romances were more her line.

"Why don't you write one yourself?" she said.

Walter stared. "Me?"

"Why not? You know all the plots inside out. I'm sure you could think up something original."

He shook his head. "It wouldn't be ethical. I'm one of the judges."

"That's easily remedied: stand down."

The more Walter thought about it, the more he liked the idea. He certainly knew every murder method, from rare South American poisons with "no known antidotes" to air embolism by injection. And it wouldn't actually be cheating. Indeed, he'd be doing his readers a service. . . . Reggie would stand in for him on the panel of judges; he would ring him in the morning.

That night, typing up the story, he lost all track of time and it was past 3 a.m. when he'd sewn up all those loose ends. He typed a pseudonym on the title page and left it ready for posting.

At the club, members were telling one another incredulously: "Heard about old Walter? He's snuffed it."

Even the old codgers dozing in the library roused themselves to hear how his wife had found him dead in bed. She'd been unable to wake him when she took him his early morning cup of tea and, thinking he'd had a stroke, had phoned the doctor.

"Poor old Walter," Reggie murmured. "He was the last person I'd have thought to be a heart case."

"Well, that's what they think it was," the club secretary said. "The actual cause of death is a mystery, I'm told; but the pathologist definitely rules out foul play.

"His wife said he'd been burning the midnight oil a lot lately. Overdid it, I suppose. Must have been quite a shock for her."

Jane was lolling in a chair on the sundeck, carrying out doctor's orders. He'd told her she needed a complete change, to get over the shock. "A Mediterranean cruise for you, Mrs Oates. And don't be in a hurry to pick up the threads again."

Walter hadn't been wealthy, she reflected; but with his life insurance and the sale of the house. . . . It had hurt, at first, finding out about Miss Tewsland. Now it didn't seem to matter.

Gino, a young Italian steward, had been flirting with her for days. She had almost forgotten what it was like . . . having a man look at her that way.

"Why don't you bring a bottle of champagne to my cabin, Gino?"

"Si, Signora."

"And Gino—bring *two* glasses."

"Pronto, Signora," he smiled.

In her shoulder-bag was a typescript. She took it out and tore it up; then she dropped the pieces over the side of the ship.

Too bad about Walter, she thought. He would have won the competition hands down. His method was diabolically clever, yet so simple. It was a pity she couldn't tell anybody, but she might need to use it again. . . .

TIME SPENT IN RECONNAISSANCE

Ted Allbeury

JULIE PEYTON WAS twenty-two, with dark hair, big brown eyes, a neat nose and a soft gentle mouth. She sat in the small cubicle with the earphones on, watching the dials on the tape recorder and looking up from time to time at the digital clock on the wall.

In the next room Peter Harvey was interrogating the Russian. Grinding away, asking the usual questions about meeting places, dates, names, who controlled him, where did he do his training? Then he'd go back over the same questions again. One of her duties was to note the discrepancies, the hesitations and evasions. Peter would probably notice them himself but she was there, or one of the other girls, as a back-up. When you couldn't see the person's face it gave an extra awareness of what they said.

It still seemed unbelievable to her. This rambling stately home not far from London. Set in its own grounds in the quiet countryside so that at night she could hear owls and, in the spring, the bleating of new-born lambs. Discreet guards patrolled the grounds and there were surveillance and security devices everywhere. Inside, the barred windows of the basement, and the officers who could interrogate in almost every language in the world. And the steady flow of suspects and defectors laying out their tatty lives like offerings at a jumble sale. It all seemed a long way from college and the sixth form at Tunbridge Wells Grammar School for Girls.

Her father had always said that it was all very well to get a degree in some foreign language. But not Russian. How on earth would she earn a living from speaking Russian? Better get yourself a proper skill like shorthand and typing, he'd said. Mind you, he'd done the decent thing and paid for the crash course in what they called "secretarial skills". She had never told him what she did in her job.

She had still been on the secretarial course when she got the letter. It was from an address near Trafalgar Square. Would she like to come for an interview for a job in a government department where her Russian could be used?

There had been two men at the interview. One talking, one listening and watching. She was conscious of doing very badly. It was almost as if they didn't believe anything she said. There was nothing they said that was actually rude, but she disliked both of them long before the interview was half-way through. At the end of two hours, to her amazement, they offered her the job when she had finished her secretarial course.

There was no doubt that Peter Harvey was good looking when he was relaxed. She liked him; admired his obvious talent, but she had reservations. The hard lines of his mouth when he was interrogating, the half-closed eyes as he listened to the answers, disbelief so obvious on his face. But it was fair to say that that was what he was there for. Intelligence officers were trained to be like that. She remembered what they'd said on her course: "Everybody tells lies about something. It pays to find out what it is." And the course for the interrogators lasted for months, not the three weeks she had had. But give him his due, he was always amiable and friendly with her.

They had been going out together a couple of times a week for the last few months and he made it very clear that he liked her. She had taken him home once and she smiled to herself as she remembered her mother's comment: "A nice-looking young man, very polite and all that. But I wouldn't want to meet him on a dark night." For her mother the whole male world was divided into those men who she would or wouldn't like to meet on a dark night. But her mother had no idea what Peter's job was. She didn't even know what her daughter's job was. Secretary in a small government department was what they had suggested she said and she'd stuck to it.

When Peter Harvey walked into the ops room he looked around for the girl. There was only Daphne Cooper.

"Where's Julie?"

"She's gone into town. She handed over to me about five minutes ago. She'll be back for your next session after lunch."

"What bus did she catch?"

Daphne shrugged. "I think she cadged a lift."

"Who from?"

"I've no idea."

Harvey walked down the corridor to the internal phone, picked it up and dialled two numbers.

"'Is that transport? . . . is Captain Palmer's car in the garage? . . . I see . . . when did he leave? . . . No, I just wanted to check if he was around . . . Thank you, Sergeant."

He put back the receiver and his hand shook with suppressed anger. Palmer was a captain. In his late thirties. His immediate superior. A quiet man who adopted a fatherly approach to all the girls. They all liked Palmer. The reliable one, the shoulder to cry on. He and Palmer had had a quite good relationship until Julie came along. He was sure that Palmer had his eye on her. Probably impressing her with his superior rank. And making clear that Harvey was just one of his juniors.

He finished the afternoon session at five and walked into her small annexe.

"What did you think of him?"

"Beginning to sound like a 'plant'."

"Why?"

"He talked about meeting his contact at the Albert Theatre when he meant the Albert Hall. If he'd actually been there he'd have known its proper name. Said he was born and brought up in Moscow. But he's got a Georgian accent when he's tensed up."

"Anything else?"

"He gave the same two dead-letter drops and at least one recognition sign that have been used before in phoney cover stories."

He smiled. "Did you get your shopping done at lunchtime?"

"Yes, thanks."

"How did you manage to get there and back in an hour?"

"Hey, Peter. What is this—an interrogation? What I do in my lunch hour is nobody's business but mine."

"I'm sorry. I'd better get moving."

She looked up at his face and said softly, "Don't get huffy, Peter. I like you, and I admire the way you do your job, but I. . . ."

He interrupted. "I know what you mean. I apologize. How about I take you down to the coast on Sunday and we can relax and have a meal?"

She smiled. "OK. Let's do that."

At the weekly meeting Captain Palmer had gone over that week's interrogations with both of them.

"Any views on Malik, Peter?"

"There's a lot in his story that doesn't hang together. But what's really significant is that what he's told us has all been things that we know already. And it's all rather old hat, from last year rather than current stuff. Our experience of genuine defectors is that they're ready to come clean right up-to-date. All the questions I've put to him about his activities in the last few months have been evaded or he's given very vague answers."

"What was your impression, Julie?"

For a moment she hesitated. It wasn't usual to ask the opinion of an assistant unless the interrogating officer initiated it himself. She knew that Peter Harvey would have noticed and been ruffled by it.

"I think Peter's right, sir."

Palmer looked at Harvey. "How much longer do you want to give him?"

"I think I'll leave him alone for a week or ten days, do some research on what he's said so far and then have another couple of days with him."

"OK. Will you notify the duty scheduling officer tonight?"

Harvey made his point. "I'll get Julie to do it after the meeting—sir."

Captain Palmer had looked up sharply at the over-emphasized "sir". Palmer wasn't sure why it had been done. It was meant to be insolent but he classified it as juvenile. Showing off for some unknown reason.

They sat on the beach after lunch. The sun was pleasantly warm and they sat watching the sailing boats tacking and weaving round the buoys in what was obviously some local regatta.

He was resting his chin in his hands, his elbows on his drawn up knees and she said softly, "What are you going to do when your six years are up?"

He shrugged. "I don't really know. Maybe I'll sign on again provided I've had a promotion."

"What did you do before?"

"Cambridge for the languages. And a year teaching." He half smiled. "Not very successfully."

"Do you like interrogating people?"

"Depends who they are. If they're trying it on, like friend Malik, I like breaking them down. But some are pretty boring, as you know." He paused and looked at her. "What are you going to do?"

"Have four children. Two boys, two girls. A golden retriever and a thatched cottage in the country."

He smiled. "You're a romantic."

"What's wrong with that?"

He shrugged. "Nothing. I guess it's OK for girls."

"Why not for men?"

"Men have to deal with reality. The real world."

"And what *is* the real world?"

"It's where people lie and cheat. Where you have to look out for yourself. Make sure they don't put one over on you."

"D'you really believe that?"

"Of course I do."

She was silent for several minutes and then she said, "Tell me about your parents. Where do they live?"

"My father is a bank manager. Lives in Leicester. Well, just outside."

"And your mother?"

She probably wouldn't have noticed the moment's hesitation if it hadn't been for her training.

"She's just a housewife. Very beautiful. Very talented."

"Talented at what?"

"She plays the piano. Could have been a concert pianist."

It was an evening almost a week later, when they were the only staff playing tennis, and they sat drinking a Coke in the

small cedar-wood shelter facing the courts, that she asked him
if he had had a girlfriend back home.

"Nobody special."

"Did you go to dances and parties a lot?"

"No. I was always working."

"Were you happy as a child?"

He frowned and said, "Why are you asking all this?"

"I'd just like to know. You're my friend, so I'd like to know
about you."

He half smiled. "I'm sorry I was sharp." He paused. "And
I'm glad you said I'm your friend."

"Were you an only child?"

"Yes."

"Maybe that's why you're like you are."

"Oh. And how am I?"

Julie sighed. "You're a loner, and sometimes I think you're
lonely as well. If you'd had an unhappy love affair, that could
have done it. If it isn't that, then somebody must have done
something to you."

"Another amateur psychologist from the interrogation
course, eh?"

She laughed softly. "No. Not really. Anyway I think you'll
be a nice man when you're bit older and you've learned to
trust people."

"Why is trusting people always considered a virtue?"

"Well isn't it?" And she turned to look at his face.

"I don't see it as good or bad. Why get involved so that you
have to decide one way or another. Just be independent . . .
and then you won't be disappointed."

"That means you'd never love someone."

"How do you make that out?"

"Loving somebody means putting your head on the block
and handing them the chopper, hoping they won't ever use it."

He had gone into the dining room as soon as the interrogation
finished. He'd hoped to see her there and take her to the
cinema. He had booked one of the pool cars the day before to
make sure that he could take her out. His own car was being
repaired. Mrs Fisher was the only one in the dining room.

"Have you seen Julie at all, Mrs Fisher?"

"She asked me to tell you that she had to leave early. She had a telephone call. Her mother's poorly. She's gone to see her."

He walked angrily to his office and phoned the transport section.

"I'm looking for Captain Palmer. Is his car there?"

"No, sir. He left about twenty minutes ago."

"Was he able to contact Miss Peyton before he left, d'you know?"

"Yes. She was with him when he left."

"Thanks."

He slammed the phone down angrily. The lying little bitch. And that creep Palmer.

As Palmer drove through the outskirts of Bromley he asked her, "How much further?"

"About five miles."

"Don't worry, Julie. We'll soon be there." He paused. "How do you get on with the bright young man?"

"OK . . . I quite like him. But he seems a very closed up sort of fellow."

"What's that mean?"

"He's terribly suspicious."

"That's probably because of his job. We train interrogators to be suspicious."

"He says everyone tells lies."

"They do." Palmer shrugged. "They may be small lies, white lies, social lies. Making themselves more important than they really are." He paused. "What did he tell you about his parents?"

"He said his father was a bank manager."

"And his mother?"

"Just that she was very beautiful and a very talented pianist."

Palmer sighed. "Take a tip from me. Never talk about his mother."

"Why not? He's obviously very fond of her."

"Momma Harvey walked out on her husband and son when the boy was eight years old. She wasn't beautiful, but she was pretty. She was a stripper before she married and she went off with the manager of a club. He threw her out two years later.

She was passed around the third-rate clubs for three more years and finally she ended up in a unit for alcoholics in St Albans. Literally ended up. She died there."

"God, how terrible. Does he know all this?"

"Oh yes. He knows."

"No wonder he made up that story."

"You mean no wonder he lied."

"If it's a lie, it's a forgivable one."

"He could have just said that she was dead."

"You're awfully hard on him."

Palmer smiled. "I'm not. I was just testing your reactions. Character probing."

"And what did you find?"

"A generous mind. A sympathetic heart. You'll do."

At breakfast the next morning Palmer took his coffee over to the table where Harvey was sitting alone. As he sat down he said, "You look as though you didn't get much sleep last night, Peter."

"I didn't." He glanced at Palmer as he said, "And how was your evening out?"

"It wasn't improved by your telegram."

"She showed it to you, did she?"

"No. But I read it."

"That was a bit off, wasn't it? Reading other people's private mail."

"Was it really necessary? The people at her Post Office will have read it." He looked directly at Harvey's face. "What were those elegant words: 'Dear Julie—You're a lying bitch. I've had enough, Peter Harvey.'" He paused. "Charming."

"She *is* a lying bitch and you know it. She swanned off with you instead of me. She had a date with me. Left a message saying her mother was ill or something."

For a moment Palmer was silent and then he said quietly: "Maybe it's time you had a change of job, Peter. Your work seems to be getting mixed up with your private life."

"What's that mean?" The younger man's aggression was all too obvious as he spoke.

"You have to spend your working hours suspecting people.

Looking for their lies. Digging holes for them to drop into. You're beginning to do the same in your private life."

"You mean I should be the normal male sucker with girls?"

Palmer shook his head. "No. I mean that the people you interrogate are already suspect. Your friends aren't suspects . . . or shouldn't be."

Harvey's voice was shrill with suppressed anger and indignation. "For Christ's sake. She broke a date with me to go swanning off with you. If you don't really believe me, ask her."

"I can't unfortunately. She's not here." Palmer looked at Harvey's face. "I wouldn't ask her anyway."

"Where is she? She's got no leave due."

"You could end up quite a bright fellow, Harvey. But you've got a lot to learn. Learn the lesson that's staring you in the face right now."

"And what lesson is that?"

"That if you want to find out if somebody's telling you lies, you actually have to find out. Not just assume that they're lying because it suits you to think so."

"I don't get it."

Palmer looked across the room and then back at the young man as he said quietly: "Her mother was already dead when we got there. Julie's staying on for the funeral."

The shock on Peter Harvey's face was instant and obvious. "Oh my God," he whispered. "How terrible."

Palmer waited until the news had sunk in and then said: "Why don't you go up and see her? She's much in need of a shoulder to cry on."

"God, I couldn't face her. Not after that bloody telegram."

Palmer reached inside his jacket and took out a folded piece of paper. "Here. Take it. There's your telegram. She never saw it. I took it from the boy and opened it in case it was something that needed dealing with. I saw what it said and I saw it was from you. I thought it might be better to keep it." He paused. "You can take a forty-eight hour pass and a warrant. Get it from the clerk and I'll sign it." He said softly, "And if it helps you, I never was a rival. I'm married. Happily married. Julie knew that. She'd had a look in my 'P' file. And she met my wife the other day when I took her to town. Always remember that old army precept, Peter—Time spent in reconnaissance is seldom wasted."